Outwand

By John Peel

Dragonhome Books
New York

Dragonhome Books, New York
ISBN# 9780615767376

John Peel

Outwand

Prologue: One Year Ago

Andrea Ballard awoke groggy, her head hurting, her shoulder in pain, and her nostrils filled with the stench of blood and gasoline. She shook her head in an attempt to clear it, and then wished she hadn't as jagged pain lanced through her body. She opened her eyes and looked around.

And again, wished she hadn't. The darkness was pierced by wavering lights, and she suddenly remembered where she was – in the family car. Her shoulder hurt because the seat belt was cutting into it. Her head hurt because she'd slammed it into the head restraint of the driver's seat in front of her. She reached up to her forehead, and winced as she touched a very sensitive wet spot. Bringing her fingers down in front of her aching eyes revealed they were covered in her own blood. She wanted to throw up, but she knew that there was something important to do first.

Memory overwhelmed her for a moment. Night, driving down the highway. Mom and her brother, Mark, in the front, she behind. Conversation, then lights heading straight at them. Mom had swerved, there had been a horrible sound, and Andrea had been flung forward –

She couldn't have been unconscious more than a couple of minutes! She'd hit her head in the crash, but otherwise she was reasonably okay. But what about Mom and Mark? They were in front of her and they would have taken the brunt of the crash...

Andrea reached forward, dizzily, and felt around. Mom was still in her seat, unmoving. Mark seemed to have slumped forward.

Gasoline! Now Andrea realized what her fuddled brain had been trying to tell her! The stench of gasoline meant that there was a leak – probably a big one. One small spark could ignite the car into a lethal fireball. She had to get out, and then help her Mom and brother.

She slapped at the seat belt release button. At first she thought she was still too stunned to get it right, but then she realized that the release simply wasn't working. As her eyes adjusted to the poor light, she

5

could see that their car was badly buckled and in places there was jagged metal and shattered window glass. Her belt must have been damaged in the crash, and she was now trapped in her seat...

Oh, god... Her mind was coming back to normal now, and she knew she might not have more than seconds to get free. The gasoline could ignite at any moment... She needed to cut through the seat belt, but with what? Then she remembered the shopping. Mom had been to the crafts store for sewing supplies, and one of the items had been new scissors... Andrea looked frantically around, and saw the bag jammed under Mom's seat. Stretching was hard. The unmoving seat belt now cut nastily into her flesh if she tried. So close, yet she couldn't get her hand to it... She wanted to scream, but couldn't spare the time.

Her foot! She reached out with her left foot – hardly comprehending that her shoe was missing – and managed to grab the bag. It took some work, but she managed to drag the bag out from under the seat. Mom had an irritating habit of tying shopping bag handles together so that nothing would fall out. It usually annoyed her, but Andrea was glad of the habit this time – it had kept the scissors in the plastic bag. She dragged the bag close enough to grab it and rip it open. Then she tore the scissors from their packaging, and used them to saw through the belt.

Finally, it ripped, and she was free. Still holding the scissors, she tried opening her door. It wouldn't move... She looked closer and saw that the frame had buckled in the crash. Outside the car was a large tree that Mom must have side-swiped. It had dented the whole passenger side of the car. There would be no getting out of this door.

Andrea had another moment of panic, and then she realized that if *this* door was damaged, then obviously the one on the other side hadn't hit anything... She scrambled across the seat and hit the door release.

The door creaked open, and she half-fell, half-stumbled out.

The gas stench was even worse here. The tank was on the passenger side of the car, and must have ruptured in the crash. She stood, giddily, and tried to get her bearings. They were in a slight dip off the expressway, close to the tree they had hit. Bits of glass and metal littered their path, but, amazingly, one headlight was still working, which explained why there was at least a low level of light. She could hear other cars going past, and considered for a moment trying to stop one. But did she have time? And wouldn't that be more dangerous – trying to wave down a car speeding past? She might get hit.

Instead, she wrenched open the driver's door. Mom was slumped in the seat, blood all over her head. Oh God! Was she dead? Andrea dropped the scissors and fumbled to find her mother's pulse. To her intense relief, it was beating – a bit faintly, but regularly. She was alive, at least, even if she was hurt. Andrea stabbed at the seat belt release, and breathed a sigh of relief as this one worked.

Mom fell out of the seat, onto Andrea. They both went down in a pile. Andrea struggled free of Mom's dead weight, and then grabbed both of her mother's wrists. She knew you weren't supposed to move an injured person, in case you added to their injuries. But in this case, she had no choice – there was much more chance that the car might explode in flames.

There was the screech of brakes, and she heard a car door open. Feet pounded over, and then two young men were with her.

"Jeez!" one exclaimed. "You're really lucky."

"Yeah, I *feel* lucky," Andrea grunted. The man helped to take some of her mother's weight, and to drag her clear.

"Is there anyone else?" the other man asked.

"My brother," she said, agony in her voice. "He's in the passenger seat." The man nodded, and rushed to the car.

"Watch out!" the one helping Andrea called. "This place reeks of gas."

"I'm okay," the second man called back.

The first man and Andrea managed to half-carry Mom back to the stopped car. The young man pulled out a cell phone and started dialing. "We saw you in our headlights," he explained, waiting for a response to his call. "I don't think any other cars did." Then 911 answered, and he started giving details.

Andrea didn't listen. As soon as she was sure Mom was as comfortable as was possible, she started back for the car. The man on the phone yelled out to her, but she ignored him. She had to help save Mark. He was her older brother, but it was her job to look out for him. He was so impractical at times she was used to doing things for him. She stumbled back to the car and saw that the second man had managed to drag Mark partly out through the driver's side door. She hurried to give him a hand, and together they carried Mark away from the car. Andrea had her arm around Mark's waist, and it felt wet and sticky. Had he soiled himself in the crash? It was an icky thought, but she didn't care right now. Saving his life was all that mattered.

They made it back to the other car, and laid Mark gently down on the grass verge. They were about thirty yards from their car now.

"You okay?" the second man asked her, looking at her in concern. "There's blood on your head."

"Just a bang," she replied, though it *did* hurt. She looked at her hand, covered in blood, and then down at Mark. It was blood that she'd felt on his back, and she saw it was still leaking from her brother. "Oh, God, he's bleeding," she gasped.

"Ambulance on the way," the first man assured her. "And a cop should be here any time. It'll be okay."

As she looked around, another man came stumbling out of the trees. It was only then that Andrea saw there was another car down in the ditch beside the highway. The car that had almost run into them! This must be the driver! She'd completely forgotten about the other car...

"Wha's up?" the man called out, stumbling. "Jeez. Some party." Then he collapsed.

"He's hurt," she said, feeling terrible that she hadn't even thought about him. The second man had run to help the fallen man. He looked back at them.

"He's not hurt," he called. "He reeks of alcohol. He's drunk."

A drunken driver... Driving on the wrong side of the highway. It was *his* fault. Andrea felt her rage rising. She stumbled back to her feet, wanting to go and punch and kick this jerk for almost killing her family.

At that moment, Mark awoke. He groaned, and she fell back to her knees beside him. "I feel awful," he moaned. "Andrea, what's happened?"

"We were in a car accident," she told him. She wanted to hug him, to reassure him, but she was afraid she might hurt him. She was just so glad he was alive and okay! "An asshole drunk ran us off the road."

"Mom?" he asked. "How's Mom?"

"Unconscious, but she's alive. There's an ambulance on the way, and they'll check her out."

"Yeah." Mark struggled to move.

"Don't!" Andrea warned him. "Wait! Let the EMT guys examine you. You could hurt yourself."

"My legs," he gasped. "I can't feel my legs." He grabbed at her in panic. "Andrea, I can't feel my legs!"

Chapter One

Andrea felt a thrill – again! -- as she moved down the sloping pathway and the castle came into view. Her third visit this week, and she still couldn't get over how magnificent and desolated it looked.

"Tintagel Castle," Carter Tremaine said softly, as he walked beside her. "Birthplace of King Arthur, the Once and Future King of all England..." Just the thought of that ancient story warmed Andrea against the nipping wind that always seemed to blow about the ruins.

"Oh, give me a break from that tourist rubbish," her brother Mark complained, rolling his eyes. "That's just so much historical nonsense, and you know it. There was most likely never a King Arthur, and certainly nothing like the Knights of the Round Table. It's just crap you locals spew out to bring in the tourist dollars."

Andrea glanced at her brother as he sat and scowled in his wheelchair. Some of what he had said was nothing but his own bitterness spilling out, but there was a certain amount of truth in his words. She'd persuaded him to take the "Round Table" exhibition the day before, and it had proven to be nothing but cheerful exploitation of the local legends, with mock chairs and a quite-recent reconstruction of what the Round Table "might" have looked like. "Not unless they had modern paints in the fifth century," Mark had muttered.

Once, Mark had been bright and happy, but that had ended, like so much, a year ago. The day that a drunk driver had cut off their car and sent them into the tree beside the road... When she wasn't careful, Andrea found images from that night flashing through her mind and haunting her life. And all she'd suffered were some scratches and bruises, soon healed. Mark, however, had taken the brunt of the impact from the crash, and a piece of jagged metal had slashed into his back...

Blood everywhere, and Mark, mercifully, unconscious once again when the police, fire brigade and ambulance had carefully carried him to the ambulance from the crash site.

Andrea's memories of that night were washed in red – the

flashing lights of the emergency vehicles, the terribly huge puddle of blood spreading from her brother's broken body and finally the flames as their car had caught fire. She'd been hysterical, afraid that Mark was going to die – how could he possibly live, having lost all of that blood, and with that wickedly sharp piece of metal sticking into his body so deeply?

But Mark had lived, though there were plenty of times he'd cursed the fact. "If only I'd never woken up," he'd complain. "To t̲his!"

This was the wheelchair he needed to be mobile now. The crash had severed the nerves in his spine, making his legs completely useless. The doctors couldn't even manage to be optimistic: he would never, ever walk again. Zero chance. It was the wheelchair for life.

And Mark had been so active – football, basketball, running – and so full of life. He was an older brother Andrea had always looked up to and admired. If there had been one person in the world she wanted to be like, it was Mark. Well, Mark as he used to be. Now his emotions were twisted far worse than his body, and his joy had less chance of ever walking again than his legs.

It had poisoned his life, and it had poisoned the family's life. Mom had been driving, and she blamed herself over and over for what had happened. The fact that the police had prosecuted and convicted the other driver of being drunk and causing the accident was of no consolation to her. She'd withdrawn as much as Mark had done, only she withdrew completely from the family.

The divorce was only a month old, and it still hurt them all. Andrea and Mark, of course, but especially Dad. He'd fought and pleaded with Mom the whole time, trying to save the marriage and the family, and only succeeded in making her more determined to flee and hide herself from the people whose lives she knew she was shattering for a second time. Dad couldn't face being in the family house with the family so broken up and apart; so when he'd been offered the chance to come to England, he'd leaped at it like a tiger on its prey, hoping it would offer them all – what? Peace? Redemption? Reunification?

If so, it wasn't really working. Oh, Dr. David Ballard, visiting professor of Medieval Studies was doing fine at the University. He was losing himself in both teaching and researching the Middle Ages, which he'd always loved. Unlike back home in the United States, here history was all around, dating back thousands of years. Andrea loved the way that you could walk down a perfectly normal-looking street and stumble across Roman ruins dating back two thousand years. In the States anything dating back to the previous century was considered ancient – here it was considered "modern rubbish"! Dad was in his element. He was living his work every day and almost managing to interest himself in life again.

And Andrea herself was enjoying it. Living with the Tremaine family in their old-but-modernized farmhouse was a grand adventure. It had been built in the Sixteenth Century, though thankfully modernized. She loved England – what parts she'd seen of it – and she liked the family. And the Tremaine's son, Carter, seemed to have taken an interest in her, too, which was an added bonus. He hadn't seen many American girls, and certainly not this close-up. He'd been surprised that she wasn't a Valley Girl, constantly spouting "like, totally, fer shure" and whatever, which amused her. He had such TV-bred views of Americans! But he was cute, and fun, and willing to spend time with her and show her around. And he knew all the local stories, and was always interested in sharing them with her.

The only real problem, as ever, was Mark. He loathed England, he loathed Tintagel, Cornwall, and he loathed the local food – even the huge, delicious Cornish pasties that Andrea couldn't get enough of.

He especially loathed the fact that nothing was level here. "Handicap accessible" was a bit of a joke – if you weren't handicapped – because for hundreds of years nothing had been constructed with wheelchairs in mind. In the past, if you were as injured as Mark had been, you simply died. Mark always claimed he wished he had, and it poisoned everything for him. He'd refused to visit the castle for the first week, because it was "too rough" going down the slope. The only reason he'd given in finally was because he hated being bored more than he hated being inconvenienced. Not the jolliest of companions to have around, but Andrea had felt compelled to try and make Mark have a good time.

It was, as Carter had pointed out twice already this morning, a complete waste of effort. Mark didn't *want* to have a good time. He *wanted* to feel miserable and sick and to hate everything. "Leave him to it," Carter had urged. "Let him stew in his own juices." But Andrea couldn't bring herself to do that, even though she knew Carter's assessment was pretty much correct.

To be honest, she felt guilty that she'd survived the crash virtually unharmed and Mark had not. She felt that, somehow, she owed him for it. She knew it was silly — as silly as Mom's ideas she was at fault - but she also knew she couldn't just ignore those feelings. So she would do whatever she could to try and brighten his life. Even if he didn't want or appreciate it.

Even forcing him to agree to see the castle of Tintagel. It had taken some persuasion, since there was no way he could really visit the castle itself — it was perched atop a crumbling cliff face and only accessible via a bridge - but she felt that she and Carter could describe it well enough and portions of it were visible from the pathway and the beach below. As they moved down past the visitor center, Carter tried to explain what they were seeing.

"Long ago," he said, trying to sound distant and mysterious, "this area was well-known for its tin mines. People from as far away as Greece came here for the tin we produced. So a thriving community was formed. And with wealth came raids. So some unknown warrior king decided that a castle was needed, and that this spot was the perfect place for it." He gestured at the sight in front of them. "On this headland jutting into the Atlantic Ocean, he had his people
build a fortress to commandeer the seas. This was about 400 AD, when the Romans were leaving Britain finally, and strong local kings arose. This is the castle where King Arthur was born, and it fell into disuse after Arthur's death. By 700 AD, it was a ruin. The castle you can see now —"

"Is still a ruin," Mark complained sourly.

"-- was built during the Middle Ages," Carter continued, "around 1250 AD. That, too, fell into ruins in the Fifteenth Century. Part of the reason, as you can see, is because the headland collapsed, bringing down the castle."

This was quite clear, in fact. The old headland was now an island, and two bits of the ruins were separated by the fallen section, now spanned by a modern, flimsy-looking bridge. There was no real way for Mark to get his powered wheelchair into the castle ruins, so they were taking him, instead, down to the beach below the castle wreckage. Andrea loved looking up at the jagged remains of the stone fortress, but Mark didn't seem to be too impressed.

"The funny thing," Carter added, as they approached the beach, "is that for the longest time historians said that the medieval castle was all there was, and the stories about Arthur being born here were obviously later additions to the Arthurian saga." He grinned. "With all due respect to your father, those historians were wrong. In 1983, a fire ravaged the island, burning off the grass. Then wind blew away a lot of the topsoil, uncovering the foundations of the much-older, original castle. The stories were shown to be true, that there had been a castle here in the Arthurian period. Score one for the legends! So if the castle is true, why not the stories? Here was born Arthur, true king of all England!" He struck a dramatic, cheeky pose.

"Who probably never really existed," scoffed Mark, unimpressed. "Just because there was a moldy old castle here doesn't make the rest of the crappy story true. Knights of the Round Table, the Holy Grail, Excalibur – they're all nothing but fairy stories."

Carter finally looked like Mark's digs were getting to him. "They're *inspirational*," he replied coldly. "No fairies. Okay, I'll grant you that a lot of it couldn't be true – dragons
and all that. But *some* of it was. The whole thing wasn't invented."

"So you say," mocked Mark. "But there's no proof for any of that nonsense. I know, the castle is here, but so what? That doesn't mean that Arthur was real, or even that he was here even if he did live. It's just fables and stories to tell the babies when you tuck them in at night. And while I may need tucking in at night, I don't need fairy stories to make me sleep. A couple of pills work much better, and they're *real*."

Hoping to head off any more arguing, Andrea said brightly: "And here's something that's real, too: the waterfall." She loved this beach, more than any she'd ever known. It was too cool here generally to sunbathe, but it was otherwise lovely. To the left was the fanged rock that held the castle; more rocks were scattered about the area and in the waves. But behind them was a cliff face, and down this came the waterfall.

It wasn't terribly spectacular, of course, since it only fell something like sixty feet, but it was unexpected and very pretty. She'd never been to another beach with a waterfall at all, so this was delightful.

Mark just sniffed. "It's pathetic," he complained. "They have better ones in Hawaii – where I'd much rather be than this dismal country. And I'm having trouble with my wheelchair on this sand."

Andrea bit back her anger; getting mad with her brother wouldn't help at all. She had to humor him, and hope that his mood would improve. She gestured instead at the rocky outcropping upon which the castle sat. At the base was a cave that ran through the entire promontory. "Merlin's Cave," she said. "It's only there at low tide, and you can go through it."

"Why would I want to go through it?" Mark sighed. "This is just as dull as everything else in this crummy town." With an effort, he turned his wheelchair around. "I want to go back now. I can be bored just as easily back at the house."

"Put some effort into it," Carter grumbled. "If you try a bit, you might start enjoying yourself, you know. And make
life a bit more pleasant for the rest of us."

Mark glowered at the English boy. "Try sitting in this chair for a year, and see how much *you* enjoy it."

"Feeling sorry for yourself won't help," Carter insisted. It would do no good, because Andrea and her father had both tried talking like that to Mark, but Carter had to discover this for himself.

"*Nothing* will help," Mark said bitterly. "My legs are dead, and that's it. I only wish I was as well."

"You might as well be," Carter growled.

"Yes," Mark agreed. "I might as well be. And until I am, I'm going back to the house."

"What a pain in the arse," Carter muttered, but Mark heard him – as Carter had probably intended.

"You want a real pain in the butt? Try this wheelchair. I'm probably lucky I don't feel anything below the waist, because I'd be sore

15

all over if I could."

Andrea sighed; she had felt so sure that even Mark would be taken by the beauty of this place. But, once again, she'd been proven wrong. She prepared herself to go back with him, in case he needed help that he'd never ask for, when Mark suddenly stopped, a confused expression on his face. "What is it?" she asked.

"I... don't know..." Mark scowled, and looked around. "There's..." he shook his head and started to wheel forward again. Then he stopped. "I just feel..."

"Sick?" she asked, anxiously.

"No..." He looked around and abruptly moved his wheelchair across the wet sands with surprising ease. He was heading away from the cave and waterfall, out towards the sea. Puzzled, Andrea exchanged a glance with Carter, and then they both followed Mark. He stopped suddenly, and there was excitement in his eyes -- for the first time since the crash.

"It's here," he said, firmly, gesturing down at the sand beneath his wheels. "I can feel it."

"What is?" Carter asked.

"I'm... not sure," Mark answered in a whisper. "But I can *feel* it, right here, just below me. Get it for me."

"Get it?" Andrea was confused.

"Dig!" her brother ordered, gesturing at the sand.

Carter shot her a *what's-wrong-with-him-now?* look. "With our bare hands?" he asked sarcastically.

"With anything you can," Mark replied urgently. "Just *dig*. It's *here*." There was complete conviction in his voice and a focus he hadn't shown in a long time. Even if there didn't seem to be a logical reason for it.

Andrea realized that they had better humor him. "Maybe we should go and buy a bucket and spade?" she suggested. "And build him a sandcastle while we're at it?"

"Don't be stupid," her brother snapped. "This isn't a game; it's serious. You have to dig, here and now!"

Carter shrugged. "I'll go back to the tourist center," he said. "They

John Peel

know me there and they'll lend me a shovel if I ask them. I just hope they don't ask me what I want it for, because I couldn't possibly explain it." He set off back the way they had come.

"Hurry up, hurry up," Mark muttered impatiently. He was staring at the sand and drumming the fingers of his right hand on his wheelchair arm.

"Mark," Andrea said gently, "what's the matter with you? What is it?"

"I don't know," he answered without looking up. "I can just... *feel* something. Calling to me. It's down there, in the sand, waiting for me to find it..."

Andrea was starting to get worried; this was very unlike Mark. He'd never been obsessive, even before his accident. What could possibly have gotten into him? Had something affected his mind? His medications, perhaps? Bringing him down here might not have been a very good idea, after all.

It took Carter about five minutes to get back with the spade, and Andrea was relieved when he returned. Mark had been getting more and more tense the whole time, and she'd been afraid he might be heading for some sort of a breakdown. The moment he saw Carter, Mark yelled: "Here! Dig! Now!"

What on earth was possessing him?

"All right, all right," Carter muttered. He sank the shovel into the wet sand and started to dig. The work soon made him sweat, but Mark urged him on. Feeling guilty, Andrea insisted on taking a turn to give Carter a break. It was hard going, especially since she had no idea why Mark was acting this way, or what it was they were supposed to be looking for. There couldn't possibly be anything of interest here. She tried to question him, to point out that this was silly, but he just ignored her and insisted that they keep digging. Carter took back the spade from her with a sigh and continued.

The hole was about four feet deep, and Mark leaned forward in his chair, peering eagerly downward. "Keep going," he urged Carter.

Carter scowled at him and wiped his brow. "This is almost deep enough to tip him into," he said to Andrea. "I'll bet we could bury him

17

faster than he could dig his way out." Andrea could understand the wish – Mark was being more of a pain than normal.

"How much further do we do this?" she asked her brother.

"Until we find it!"

"There's no *we*," Carter complained. "Just *us*. You're just sitting there, acting crazy."

"Don't waste your breath," Mark snapped. "Dig!"

"There's nothing here!" Carter exploded, throwing down his tool. "It's just sand on a beach!"

"It's there," Mark insisted. "Andrea, take over!"

Andrea hesitantly picked up the shovel. Her muscles ached, and she couldn't see any point to this, other than to placate him. "What is it we're looking for?"

"I don't know," he admitted. "But I can *feel* it."

Carter bunched up a fist. "You'll feel this in a bit."

"Carter, please," Andrea begged. The English boy shrugged and stood aside. With a sigh, she continued to dig down. It seemed stupid and pointless, and she could only hope that her brother would lose interest soon.

Another foot down and the blade struck something.

"Hey!" she exclaimed.

"It's probably just a rock," Carter said, gesturing around. "This place is littered with them."

It hadn't felt like a rock. She dug a little more carefully, and realized that there *was* something here. Carter jumped down and took the tool from her.

"I'll do it," he said gently. "You look like you need a break."

That was true enough. She clambered out of the hole, sticky, sweaty and with sand in her feet. She wanted a shower, and she was hungry. Glancing at her watch, she saw that it was lunchtime. They'd been here hours! Digging a stupid hole! She was glad there were only a handful of tourists about, most of whom eyed them with minimal curiosity and then dismissed them.

Mark was oblivious to them and to everything but the object they were uncovering. He didn't notice the time or the people giving them odd looks. He leaned forward eagerly in the wheelchair, impatiently, but managing to restrain himself for the most part. "That's it," he breathed. "I can *feel* it..."

Carter muttered under his breath and continued to dig around the object. Despite his mood, he was clearly working carefully, uncovering...

A piece of wood.

He looked up at Mark, incredulously. "*This* is it?" he growled. "All this work for some driftwood?"

"It's not driftwood," Mark said. "Give it to me! Give it to me!"

"I'd like to break it across your head," Carter complained. Nevertheless, he pulled it from the last of the sticky sand and handed it up to the impatient boy. Mark grabbed it, brushing off the sand, and hugged it to his chest.

Andrea had to sympathize with Carter here; it obviously *was* just a lump of driftwood. It was about four and a half feet long, clearly from a branch of some tree. It was twisted and gnarled, a dark – almost black – color. One end was fatter than the other, making it look like some long, warped walking stick. Other than that, it was simply the sort of wood you found anywhere on a beach, washed up by the waves.

Yet Mark had an expression on his face she hadn't seen in more than a year. He looked happy – and more than a little feverish.

"That's it?" she asked him, disappointed.

"Yes." Mark jammed the stick onto the seat beside him and used both hands to abruptly whirl his wheelchair around. "I'm going home now. I don't want to be disturbed."

"Too late for that," Carter commented. "If you ask me, you're seriously disturbed." Mark ignored the comment and sent his wheelchair off across the beach and toward the path back.

Andrea sighed. "I suppose we'd better go after him." It would be hard work for him to wheel himself back up the pathway to the main road.

"No way," Carter said. He gestured to the hole they'd dug. "We have to fill this in again. Somebody could get hurt otherwise. Let him go off and gloat over his moldy old stick. I'll buy you lunch."

Andrea realized he was right – they couldn't leave the hole. But she felt so achy! Well, this was her fault, she supposed, for dragging Mark down here in the first place. "All right."

"It's still not too late to drag him back and bury him," Carter commented. He sounded like he was only half-joking...

Chapter Two

The sound of screaming brought Andrea abruptly awake and shaking in her bed. It was dark in her room, but a little light filtered in through the window, which she'd left slightly open for fresh air. Her heart pounded as she sat there, staring around, her ears straining for any sound. She had started to believe that the noise had been in some terrible dream when it came again, long and high-pitched. It didn't sound like a person, but perhaps some animal, screaming in fear and shock.

Andrea hesitated, and then hopped out of bed. She found her slippers, and slipped a robe over her nightie. The clock said it was just past one in the morning, so everyone should be home by now and in their beds. She couldn't imagine that she was the only one who had heard the horrible screams. Shivering, she belted her robe and went out of her room.

The Tremaine family always left a couple of lights on, since the house was over three hundred years old and had been added to over the years, so the windows were often in inconvenient places to illuminate anything. It made going to the bathroom easier having the nightlights, and it helped Andrea find her way downstairs now. There was no sign that anyone else was awake and she wasn't sure that she should rouse anyone else until she knew what for.

In the kitchen, she hesitated. Was it wise to go outside at night, with some unknown animal out there and in pain? But she couldn't bear the thought of some creature, wounded, perhaps dying, that needed help. If she did nothing, it could die slowly, and she'd never forgive herself if it was just foolish fear that kept her from helping. There were some stupid drivers in the area, and it was possible that a dog or cat out on the prowl had been hit and left for dead.

Come to think of it, where was Thor? He was the family's German Shepherd, a big, loveable rogue without a
mean bone in his body. He normally guarded the kitchen by night — nobody would get *his* food! — but there was no sign of him. The screaming

came again, a wild, ululating sound that stroked the marrow of her bones with ice, and she summoned up all of her courage to plunge out of the door.

The house had a garden in the back where Carter's mother grew a lot of her own vegetables, and a small lawn out front, facing the road. Beyond the back garden was a low hedge, then a moor stretching out to the cliff tops. The sound of the waves hitting the cliffs was faint but audible. She prayed that the animal wasn't over there; she knew better than to go near the cliffs at night and with only slippers on her feet. Besides, it was a lot more likely that the injured animal was on or near the road. Padding along, she went out of the side gate and into the road.

It felt... strange. Eerie, but in a strangely good sense. Somehow Andrea felt more alive and alert than normal. It was as if the world had taken on some odd new level of reality, one step up from how things normally were. It was a night when she wouldn't have been surprised to see fairies dancing or for a unicorn to race out of the darkness. Her senses seemed to be honed to sharpness – she could feel the soft breath of the night wind on the hairs on her arms and there was the faint scent of earth and flowers. Magic was afoot on a night like this...

There weren't many street lights, and, as always it seemed here in England, clouds covered most of the sky, so it was very dark. She could make out the grayness of the road in contrast to the blackness of almost everything else. And then a beam of light caught her, making her gasp and shield her eyes.

"Andrea?" It was Carter, and, thankfully, he swung the flashlight down, out of her face. With her heightened senses it felt as if she'd been pierced by a searchlight. "You shouldn't be out here."

"I know, but I heard those screams..."

"Yeah." Carter came closer, and she saw he was in his robe also, but with boots on his feet. "I keep hearing it, but I can't see anything."

Not even any cars. The place seemed to be deserted, completely void of life outside their small circle of light. "Where's Thor?" she asked.

"I don't know," he confessed. "He came out with me, snarled, and then ran off. I haven't been able to find him – or whatever is making that sound."

As if on cue, there came another scream. Both of them jerked, and then Carter flashed the light to the east. "It was this way," he said, but hesitated. "Maybe you should go back."

"This is the twenty-first century – it's not cool to be a chauvinist," she retorted. "I'm quite as capable as you are."

"No doubt," he agreed. "Actually, I was hoping for an excuse to go back myself. I'm sure Thor will be back as soon as he realizes he's out of sight of his food dish. Thankfully there are no cars about to hit him, after all."

"But something's hurt," Andrea pointed out. "If you're going back, give me the flashlight." She reached out a hand.

Carter pulled it back. "I'm enough of a chauvinist to want to look after you," he told her."If you're investigating, then so am I." He led the way, and Andrea felt a measure of relief. She really hadn't wanted to go on alone.

A shudder passed up her spine, and not simply from the cold. It felt... *strange* out tonight. Normally she loved the night, and would have enjoyed being out alone with a cute guy. Even under-dressed. But she couldn't shake that odd feeling about this evening, and she had no desire to do anything other than check on whatever it was that had screamed and then go home again. To the safety and warmth of her bed. And it looked like Carter felt pretty much the same way that she did. She wondered if he felt the strangeness of this night, too, but felt silly asking a question like that, especially of somebody so down-to-earth. He might laugh at her, and she didn't want that.

About a hundred yards down the road was another house, but this was dark and silent. Nobody seemed to have ventured out. There was a lonely circle of light around a lamp post, and Carter stopped, gesturing down to the tarmac.

There was a dark pool there, still wet and glistening in the light. There was a strong scent of blood... It had to have been left by whatever animal had been screaming. It almost hurt her nose to smell the sharp stench of the iron-rich blood. Carter shone his light closer, and then through the pool. There were prints in the blood. Something had followed

23

whatever had been wounded, and left the tracks as the animals moved away. Several sets of prints, large and dog-like.

"Some animal was attacked," Carter whispered. "It managed to move off, but it was chased."

"By dogs?"

He shrugged. "If so, they must have been mastiffs or something. Those prints are *huge*."

"Not Thor?" She hated the idea that big, slobbery, friendly Thor might have attacked some other animal.

"That's not him. His paws aren't that big." Carter led the way again. "In fact I've never seen dog prints that large."

"They *were* dog prints, weren't they?" Andrea asked anxiously. There was something about this night that made her unsure of anything. There was an air of... what? Uncertainty? Menace? Magic?

"What else could they be?" Carter replied. His flashlight was following the bloody tracks. They were getting thinner now, but there was still the flow of blood from the hunted creature. It felt so surreal to be walking out in the English countryside after one in the morning in her robe and slippers, following... what?

There was a sudden noise that made both of them start, until Andrea realized it was just a car engine. It had been so silent before that the motor sounded terribly loud. As they walked on, they saw the headlights from the car coming toward them down the road. Then the car stopped about sixty feet ahead of them, and the door opened and then slammed shut again.

Andrea gasped. Caught in the beams of the car's headlights, she could see that there was something in the road. It had fallen and was still, but it looked like a small mountain. She and Carter sprinted forward, curiosity overcoming fear. Andrea slowed as she got closer, stunned.

"It's a deer," Carter breathed. Andrea shook her head; she knew better than that. This wasn't just a deer. She'd seen one of these creatures before. She felt an absolute sense of certainty as she stared at the body.

If it had been standing, it would have been almost eight feet tall. It was well-muscled, and its russet-red coat must once have been sleek and glossy. Now it was matted with sweat and blood. Its bloodshot eyes protruded, wide and unstaring in death. Its throat had been ripped out, and there was a large wound on the flank. That must have been caused in the first attack, the one that had bled so much. Then its hunters had closed in and finished it off here, tearing out the throat. There were more of the massive dog-prints in the blood about the throat. But the most noticeable detail about the animal was a huge spread of horns on its large head, a spread that had to be almost five feet across at the widest point.

"It's an Irish Elk," Andrea breathed softly.

The other person there, the car's driver, glanced up from the body. "I've never seen anything like it." The voice was female, with a firmness about it, as of one used to being in charge.

"Nobody living has." Andrea was dazed. "They've been extinct since the last Ice Age. I recognize it from the skeleton I saw in the Natural History Museum in New York."

Carter shook his head. "That's not possible," he muttered.

"And an animal like this living unnoticed in England *is* possible?" Andrea demanded. On a night like this, the impossible seemed to be only too real. Well, this *was* real: she reached out and touched the beast. It was still warm, and it was definitely there. No hallucination or ghost, or anything. A real, live – well, *dead* – creature, straight out of the prehistoric past, lying in a country road...

"I'd better set up flares," the woman said. "I wouldn't want some idiot motorist driving into this. It could wreck his car."

Andrea blinked and looked at their companion. She then realized that this was a British policewoman, in a severe
black skirt and top, her hair in a bun under her cap. But she seemed efficient and nice enough as she headed for the trunk of her police car – Andrea abruptly saw this was what it was – and took out several road warning flares. As she set them in place about the body, the woman glanced at them again. "You two should be in bed," she suggested. "You're not dressed for wandering about the countryside."

"We heard a noise..." Andrea tried to explain. "This poor creature being hunted, obviously."

"Well, there's nothing you can do now," the police woman

pointed out. She set the flares going, casting a reddish, hellish light across the carcass. Then she glanced around. "I'd better drive you back," she said. "After all, if there's a pack of killer dogs roaming around, I wouldn't want them to come after you next. They've killed this, but not for food — they haven't eaten any of it."

The thought hadn't occurred to Andrea, but she abruptly realized that this was a real possibility. She and Carter might have been in danger all along without realizing it. She shivered again, and realized that at least some of this was simply due to the fact that it was a cold night. "Thank you," she said gratefully. The idea of walking home again with just a flashlight for protection was not comforting.

"Maybe you should get into the car," the police woman suggested. "Just in case." She smiled comfortingly. "Besides, it has to be warmer in there. I just have to call in a quick report and then we can be off." She joined them inside the small car, and Andrea noticed that she locked the door. Then she used her radio. "This is car 18," she said. "Officer Davies." When the station acknowledged, she informed them about the carcass, and asked for it to be collected. "Plenty of meat on the bones," she added, and then signed off. She glanced in the back where Andrea and Carter were sitting. "Right, let's get you two back to your home."

The drive was short, and they saw and heard nothing else. Officer Davies nodded as she saw the house. "You're the Tremaine boy," she commented. "And you must be one of the visiting Yanks."

"Andrea Ballard," Andrea said, extending her hand.

"Blodwen Davies," the police woman said, shaking. "Well, I hope this doesn't put you off England."

"No," Andrea said, honestly. "Actually, it makes it more intriguing."

"Well, go to bed now," Officer Davies said. "Puzzle it over in the morning. Good night." She sat watching them until they reached the house, and Andrea felt comforted. It still felt very, very weird. As they let themselves in, she heard the car drive off.

"You know what's odd?" Carter said softly. "That nobody else seems to have heard what we did."

Andrea realized that this was true. Her father and brother, and both of Carter's parents were home, and, apparently, sleeping. And they had passed several houses in their hunt, and yet, apart from Blodwen Davies, had seen no one. Yet the screams had been loud enough to wake her from a deep sleep. Why had nobody else been disturbed? How could anyone have slept through those horrible sounds? And why had they not heard the dogs? Didn't hunting packs bark and snarl?

"It's been simply weird all along," she said. "An animal that died out millennia ago, dogs hunting it down, and only the three of us apparently hearing it." She shook her head. "I wouldn't be too surprised if it was gone in the morning. It's that kind of a night."

"Fey," Carter said. "Magical. As if the old times had come back again for a visit. The old spirits and gods of the woods might have returned to life for this one night."

"But is it?" she asked, anxiously. "Just the one night? Or is this only the beginning?" She didn't really know why the thought had occurred to her, but she did have this feeling tickling her brain that *something* had begun... and would go on for a while yet.

He couldn't answer that, of course. And she was afraid of what any answer given might be...

Chapter Three

When she awoke in the morning Andrea remembered every detail of her nighttime walk with an amazing clarity. She knew that it hadn't been a dream, no matter how bizarre it had been. When she went down to breakfast, Thor was back, a small mountain of fur sleeping in the kitchen. Whatever had happened in the night, it clearly hadn't changed his lazy nature. Mrs. Tremaine, by years of practice, seemed to manage to walk around him without even looking to make a pot of her ever-present tea and some breakfast. Carter was scanning the local paper at the table and glanced up.

"Nothing in the news about the deer," he told her. "But I suppose it happened too late for them to cover it. I called the police, and they told me that they've already shifted the thing." He grinned. "I expect there will be a lot of venison on the restaurant menus for the next couple of days."

"But where did it come from?" Andrea asked. She looked at his mother. "There haven't been any large deer around here, have there?"

"Not since my mother was a child," Mrs. Tremaine replied, handing her a cup of tea. "It's all this development, you know, love. It drives away the big animals. Though the foxes seem to thrive. There's one eats out of our dustbins if I don't put the lids on tightly." She shrugged. "Maybe this beast just got a bit lost."

"A *bit*?" Andrea snorted. "It's been extinct for thousands of years."

"Well, that one's only been extinct for one night," Carter joked. Then, more seriously: "Are you *sure* they're extinct?"

"Definitely." It was very disturbing. "But that animal was alive last night..." She shook her head. "There's something really strange going on."

"Well, if you want something *really* strange," Mrs. Tremaine said, "your brother isn't eating his meals. And he won't come out of his room."

Andrea scowled, partly at the change of subject – she wanted to talk about this mystery! – and partly at the news. Mark had been a problem for a while, but he always had a very healthy appetite. So much so that she'd often worried he'd get fat with all his eating and not being able to get much exercise in a wheelchair. "How long has this been going on?" she asked, worried.

"Since yesterday, when he came back from your little trip," Mrs. Tremaine replied. "He just locked himself in his room and won't come on out. And he didn't eat any food I left for him, either." She glanced at the dog on the floor. "Thor gulped it down when we had a look earlier." Thor opened an eye when he heard his name, but decided it wasn't a call for food, so he closed it again.

"I'll go check on him myself," Andrea decided, and dashed down the hallway. The front room by the door had been converted for Mark's use, so he wouldn't have to go upstairs to sleep like the rest of them. She tapped on the door. "Mark?"

"Go away!"

Well, that was pretty normal for him these days. "Are you all right?"

"I'd been fine if I was just left alone," he called back. "Go and do something mindless, and leave me in peace."

"What about breakfast?" she asked. "Shall I bring you some?"

"No."

"But you've got to eat."

"I'm on a diet, okay?" Mark was starting to sound really annoyed. "Now go away and let me get on with my work."

"Work? What work?" He wasn't making any sense.

"Just *go away*!"

Puzzled, Andrea returned to the kitchen, where Mrs. Tremaine was frying up breakfast. "He isn't being very communicative."

"In other words, he's normal," Carter said. "Leave him to it. He'll get hungry soon, even for Mom's burnt toast."

"I do not burn the toast," Mrs. Tremaine said, sniffing. Then she snatched it out from under the grill before it caught fire. "Make yourself useful and spread it." She tossed the badly-singed bread at him.

After breakfast, Andrea and Carter went outside. It seemed like another overcast day – no surprise there! – but reasonably warm. Both Dr. Ballard and Mr. Tremaine had left for work, and Andrea was feeling restless.

"What's on the agenda for today?" Carter asked her.

"I don't know," she confessed. "I'm feeling... strange today."

"Uh-oh. Maybe your brother is catching..."

"No, not like that. Like..." She couldn't find the words. "Oh, I don't know. Like I'm waiting for a letter in the mail, and it could be either very good or very bad news. You know, wanting and dreading it at the same time."

"Yeah, Tintagel can affect you like that," Carter joked. "What you need is a trip to town." He meant Launceton, the closest town of any size. "We could cruise the music stores." Then, with a condescension to her tastes: "And the book stores."

She might have been tempted some other time, but not today. "No, I think we should stay closer to home," she replied. "I can't explain it. It's just..." She shrugged. "Like electricity. There's something about the air today."

"Making everybody crazy," Carter grumbled, but not too much. "Well, whatever you want." He grinned. "How about hunting Irish elks?"

That made her smile."Could be a long hunt," she warned him. "Aside from that dead one, there shouldn't be any around these parts."

"It'll keep us busy." He gestured. "Let's check out the cliffs. They're safe by day. That's the direction it seems to have been coming from."

Andrea agreed; last night she'd felt that the elk might have come from that way. They set off, squelching on the muddy earth of the moor. It was only a matter of minutes before they came across tracks. Carter bent to examine them.

"I always wanted to be an Indian scout," he confessed. "They went thataway!" He laughed. "But even a blind man could follow these. It's definitely your elk from last night."

At least it gave Andrea one reason to like the miserable weather; the tracks had stayed fresh overnight. As Carter had said, they were simple to follow – up to the edge of the cliff. They stopped and stared at the tracks, and then at each other.

"That can't be right," Carter muttered doubtfully. "They just start at the edge of the cliff."

"I have a friend who lives in California," Andrea said. "And she tells me deer there can climb the really steep hills. Maybe this elk climbed from the beach?"

"Up this cliff?" Carter gestured down it. "It's almost sheer. And, anyway, if it had scrambled up, there would be lots of scuff-marks at the top here." He shook his head. "It's just like it was in the air and hit the ground running. The prints are quite clear – it was in mid-stride right at the edge of the cliff."

"Or as if it had come from the past into the present," suggested Andrea slowly. "The sea is wearing away at the cliffs; a few thousand years ago, they'd have been father out to sea. If that elk had been running then..."

"Animals can't travel through time," Carter objected.

"They can't survive unnoticed when they're supposed to be extinct, either," Andrea pointed out. "Not something that size, anyway. I know it's crazy to suggest it somehow ran through time, but can you think of a more sensible explanation?"

"Yes," Carter answered, firmly. "There's a government laboratory about twenty miles away. Maybe they're doing rebreeding there. You know, trying to recreate extinct species. And maybe this was one of their attempts that got away."

"What, you think they've built Jurassic Park out on the moors or something?" Andrea scoffed. "I don't think so. Besides, it doesn't explain how the tracks suddenly start here."

"It's no stupider a theory than time travel," Carter objected, sounding a trifle hurt.

Andrea immediately felt guilty. "You're right," she agreed. "I'm sorry. I just feel so strange about all of this."

"*All?*" Carter was puzzled. "What *all*? There's just a big deer."

"What about Mark and his finding that stick yesterday? And him not eating?"

"What's that got to do with anything? Look, Andrea, I like you and all, but you've got to admit that your brother isn't the nicest or most stable of individuals. The fact that's he's acting flaky just means that, for

31

him, he's normal. Which is, let's face it, unpleasant."

"Maybe." Andrea wasn't so sure, but Carter did have a point. It was possible that Mark was doing this just to get his own back at them for bothering him. She couldn't put it past him. But... Well, that answer just didn't *feel* right. There was something unearthly happening, she was sure of it, even if she couldn't describe it, or put her finger on it. It disturbed her enough to throw a cloud over the day. She knew she was no fun for Carter to be with, but he hung around with her anyway. She couldn't focus on what she was doing, though – that feeling of waiting was too strong. The day passed and she didn't know what she had done for most of it.

That evening, Mark was still in his room, refusing to come out. Carter gave a disgusted grunt when he was told to get lost. "He's not even been to the bathroom all day," he complained to Andrea. "Maybe he isn't hungry for some reason, but he ought to be coming out for that."

Andrea nodded, and banged on Mark's door herself. "Come out, or I'm coming in," she called.

"Go away!"

"No," Andrea said, firmly. "We just want to make sure you're okay."

"Didn't I tell you I was?"

"You tell us a lot of things," Andrea replied. "Mostly rude. But we want to see you for ourselves."

"You people keep annoying me," Mark complained. "Oh, if you must, then come on in."

Andrea opened the door, and she and Carter went inside. The room was a mess – which was pretty normal for
Mark. He used being in a wheelchair as an excuse for not cleaning up. The bed looked like it hadn't been slept in, though, and Mark was dressed in the same clothes he'd worn the previous day. He had a scowl on his face and the gnarled, wooden stick in his hands.

"Satisfied?" he growled. "I'm fine, I don't need anything, and I just want to be left alone."

"Don't you need to eat?" Andrea asked him. "Or a cup of tea or something?"

"Like a trip to the bathroom?" Carter suggested.

"I told you, I don't need anything." He glared at them, and gestured with the stick. "You've seen I'm okay, so now leave me in peace!"

Andrea and Carter glanced at each other, and Carter shrugged. "Okay," she agreed. "But we'll be back to check on you later, if you change your mind."

"I know you'll be back," Mark complained. "You just love to harass me, don't you? And I won't change my mind. Close the door behind you."

Outside, Carter sighed. "You know, I'd have bet your brother couldn't have gotten ruder. And I'd have lost. I don't know how the two of you can be related. You're so nice, and he's such a pill."

Andrea smiled sadly. "He didn't use to be like that. It's only since the accident."

"That was a year ago," Carter grumbled. "He's got to learn to stop feeling sorry for himself and get on with his life. There are plenty of people who are as badly off as he is, and they're cheerful enough about it."

"I'm sure he'll get over it in time," Andrea said. But there was more hope than conviction in her voice.

Her father was working in his room, so Andrea and Carter joined his parents to watch television. Andrea wasn't up to paying much attention, but she started when the TV suddenly scrambled. The sound howled and looped, and the picture broke up.

"Bloody cable company," Mr. Tremaine complained. He slapped the side of the TV set, with no noticeable effect.
"Charge you through the nose and deliver bloody awful service. It didn't use to be like this when we had the antenna. What's their number?"

"I'm sure a lot of people will call and complain about this," Mrs. Tremaine replied. But she went to the desk, obviously to hunt for the last bill. Carter turned the sound completely down on the set, which was a relief. The screaming had been very grating.

Andrea wasn't particularly bothered by the loss of the show, since she hadn't been paying it much attention anyway. She didn't even have a clue what it had been. "I guess I'll go and read in my room," she said, and opened the door to the hallway. Then she stopped, her hand still on the knob. "Carter..."

The front door, down the hallway, had a glass insert over it. In the morning, sunlight would stream inside. Now, however, greenish light flickered. It cast spectral fingers down the length of the hallway, twisting and writhing.

"What the heck is that?" Carter wondered. "Aurora? Electrical storm?"

"It could be what's making the TV act up," his mother suggested. She stood behind them, the cable bill in her hand. "Bill, come and look at this," she called back to her husband.

Carter moved to the front door and opened it. Andrea and his parents were right behind him as they walked together out of the house and stared around.

The sky lit up again, jagged lightning flashing across the heavens. Andrea shivered. There was no sign of clouds for once, and the flashes were a luminescent green, not the bright, eye-shocking yellow and white she was used to. The entire sky seemed lit, and it cast a spectral pall over the town. The green was vaguely luminescent and an unhealthy shade.

"Damned weather," Mr. Tremaine complained.

"No," Andrea answered, almost in a whisper. "It's not that. Listen: there's no thunder, just lightning. And that's impossible."

"Maybe the storm's just further off than it looks, dear," suggested Mrs. Tremaine.

"It's lighting up the whole town," Andrea pointed out. "That means it's got to be directly overhead. We should have the house rattling with thunder!"

There was another jagged flash, and they all shivered, waiting for the crash that never came.

"It's probably them damned scientists messing around again," Mr. Tremaine decided. "They're always screwing up the environment. This is probably due to global warming."

"I don't see what they could be doing to cause this," Andrea said.

"Maybe it's the aurora?" Mr. Tremaine said.

"I've seen the aurora borealis once," Andrea said softly. "It's like strands of light in the sky. Not at all like this. And it's never this far south."

"Global warming," Mr. Tremaine repeated, but with less conviction.

"Maybe it's flying saucers?" suggested Mrs. Tremaine.

"Makes as much sense as anything else," agreed Carter. "It does look like *Close Encounters*." Another silent flash glowed across the sky.

Andrea shivered, hugging herself more for comfort than warmth. They all stood just outside the house, watching the ghostly light-play.

Then she heard a sound in the distance, behind the house. "Listen! What's that?"

They all turned to try and answer her, but they were as puzzled as she was.

It sounded like a low rumble of thunder or something, but not from the sky – from the ground. It was growing louder by the moment.

"Earthquake?" suggested Carter, his face pale.

Andrea shook her head. "I've been in one in California, and it didn't feel like this." She managed a wan smile. "I know you English like to do things differently, but not this differently." The rumbling grew louder, and now she could make out individual sounds.

"It's a lot of – I don't know, *things* – on the move," Mr. Tremaine suddenly announced. "That's feet running."

He was right, Andrea realized. It sounded like she was listening to a stampede. But of *what*? Nervously, they all moved to the side of the house, to get a good look. The feeling she'd had the previous night was back, and even more intense, if anything. Her senses were alert, her brain seemed to be absolutely clear and her breathing shallow.

Something was happening once again. Something fey, like the previous night...

There was more of the green light over toward the cliffs, but a continual glow, not the flashes of lightning. It seemed to be over the sea, in the air but drawing closer to the ground.

"It *is* a flying saucer!" Mrs. Tremaine breathed. "It's landing in our back yard!"

"No," Andrea pointed out. "It's not that at all. It's.... I don't know..."

The light seemed to be pulsing or writhing, moving about as it drew closer. It took her a minute to understand why, and then the truth clicked. "It's a lot of things, moving together..."

She could start making out some of the details now. There were lights of slightly different sizes, and they seemed to be bouncing about as they moved. They were all shades of green, from light lime to almost black, all with their own luminescence. As the lights drew closer, the sound of running feet grew, too.

Then the lights hit the edge of the cliff, and the ground started to shake from the thunder of their passage. The shapes were moving with tremendous speed, and they were almost upon the four observers before it became clear what they were seeing.

They were hounds – huge, snarling, shaggy creatures, unlike any dogs Andrea had ever seen. They were man-sized and heavy-set, but with massive endurance and huge maws. She would have expected barking and howling, but they ran silently, predators after their prey – another of the massive, graceful, impossible elks. This had flecks of saliva about its muzzle, and its eyes were wide and fear-filled. It knew it was racing for its life. These figures swept past Andrea and her
stunned companions, and what followed behind was, if anything, worse.

Riders – dozens of them, on immense, powerfully-built, straining horses. The mounts strove to keep pace behind the hunting hounds, and the riders ignored everything but their prey. That was the only thing about them to be thankful for. Andrea huddled back, shaking, and felt Carter put a comforting arm about her shoulders. Except his hand was as unsteady as hers. Andrea felt certain that they *really* shouldn't draw the attention of these hunters.

The riders were all alike in some ways, and vastly different in others. Their clothing varied greatly – from leather armor to what looked like Roman togas – but everything the riders wore was all old and tattered, cloth streamers blowing behind the men as they rode, bent over their horses' necks, mouthing encouragement impossible to hear over the thunder of the hooves striking the ground. The men – Andrea believed that they were all men – had bows, or swords, or simply long knives, all bright and flashing in the ghastly light.

All of the riders were in various stages of decomposition. Flesh rotted on the pale bones, eyes gaped or were clouded; lips were stretched to impossible lengths. Clumps of hair streamed as the hunters rode, along with shreds of skin and flesh. They were all animated corpses, grimly set on their mad sport. Andrea wanted to vomit, but she didn't dare take her eyes off the terrible riders in case one of them should turn and notice her standing there.

She had no doubt that, if this happened, she would be the target of flashing sword or swift arrow. These dead men *hunted* – it was their only reason for existing still, when they should be buried and forgotten.

"Jesus, Joseph and Mary," Mrs. Tremaine breathed, crossing herself. She was shaking badly, and her voice was unsteady.

Then the hunters were past them, past the house, and into the road. The sound of their passage started to fade, and the greenish corpse-light shaded to night. Carter kept his arm about Andrea, and she suspected it was as much because he needed support to stand as to comfort her.

"The Wild Hunt," Carter gasped. "We saw the Wild Hunt."

"What's that?" Andrea asked, somewhat surprised that she had any voice left.

"It's an old myth," Carter said, babbling slightly from the shock. "Herne the Hunter leads his followers on a mad hunt across the night sky." Andrea realized she'd heard about the Hunt before, probably from her father.

"This wasn't across the night sky," Mrs. Tremaine said, a touch of anger driving the fear from her voice. "It was across my vegetable patch, the bloody hooligans!"

Andrea had been certain that what they had been observing was some kind of haunting – she remembered the old folk song she used to sing in school, "Ghost Riders In The Sky" – and had thought the Wild Hunt to be much the same – specters riding forever in a ghostly, intangible hunt. But this one had left considerable evidence of its passage. The vegetable garden was in shambles, deep gouges of hoof-prints savaging the earth. Part of the fence had been smashed by the horses, and the lawn ripped up by sharp hooves.

"It was real," Andrea breathed. Not ghosts, then – but what?

Chapter Four

"I'm going to report those maniacs to the police," Mr. Tremaine said, furiously. "Look what they've done. They'll pay for this, mark my words." He strode off toward the house, his wife following, complaining about the damage.

Andrea stared at Carter. "They've got to be joking," she finally said. "Those riders were *dead*; the police aren't going to be able to lock them up." She couldn't believe the reaction of his parents. What was wrong with them?

"If the cops are very lucky, those riders won't even notice them," Carter said grimly. "According to the legend, if they look at you and see you, then you're doomed to join the Wild Hunt yourself, riding forever with them. Even death can't stop them." he shuddered again. "And it obviously didn't."

Andrea's tattered nerves were starting to calm down again. "I'm assuming that this sort of thing doesn't happen around here every night?"

"No, generally we know how to give visitors a good time, not scare the living daylights out of them." Carter suddenly seemed to realize he still had his arm about her and let go as if she'd suddenly become impossible to touch. "That's why my folks are acting so strangely. They don't know what else to do."

"I don't know what to do, either," Andrea said slowly. "To be honest, what we just saw terrified me."

"It scared the hell out of me, too," Carter admitted. Then he glanced around. "Come on." He moved toward the street, and looked up and down the road. "I can't believe there's nobody else out here looking at it."

He was correct, Andrea saw; the road was deserted. Some of the houses had lights on, showing people were awake, but they were the only people in sight. "Maybe they have their TVs turned on really loud?" she suggested.

"Ours went out," he reminded her. "Theirs' should have, too. I don't get it."

Andrea's skin went cold. "What's even odder is that neither Dad nor Mark came out, either," she said slowly. "Why not? We heard everything quite distinctly – why wouldn't they?"

"Good question." There was nothing more out here to see, except further prints across the front lawn and the torn-up plants and clods of grass scattered from their garden across the road. They went back to the house, to discover that Dr. Ballard was now downstairs, talking with Carter's parents. He glanced up as they entered.

"You saw all of this, too?" he asked them. He looked as if he thought the Tremaines were losing their minds. He wasn't too specific, but Andrea could guess what he meant.

"Everything," she replied. "And there are hoof prints all over the front and back lawns."

"I didn't hear a thing," he confessed, surprised. "I was just reading through papers upstairs. You'd think I'd have heard whatever you all did."

"You must have been very involved," Andrea said sympathetically. Her father could forget the world sometimes when he was absorbed in his work. It was possible he was simply too absorbed to have even notice anything. "What about Mark?"

Dad shrugged. So Mark was still in his room. Normally, Andrea would have been amazed, but Mark had been acting so oddly recently that this almost seemed normal. "I'll go ask him if he heard anything," She started for his room, but paused in the hallway, and stared through the glass above the front door. "It's back," she said softly.

The others followed her gaze, and they could see a flashing redness outside the house. As they looked, there came a rapping on the door.

"You think it's the Hunt come for one of us?" Carter asked, worried.

"I don't think they're polite ghosts," Andrea replied. "They'd hardly knock." But she wasn't certain of this, of course, and made no move to answer the door. Neither did the Tremaines. After a moment, Dr. Ballard moved forward. "Dad, be careful," Andrea warned him.

He scowled as if she was being foolish – but he hadn't seen the riders, of course, and didn't understand her fears. Her father threw open the door, and Andrea gasped.

The policewoman they had met the previous night was standing there. The red light was on her car, flashing by the front gate. Andrea was so relieved that she almost collapsed.

"You called for help?" Blodwen Davies asked. She gestured at the lawn. "Looks like the work of vandals. We had a few calls from the area about noise and rowdies."

"They weren't your usual sort of vandals," Mrs. Tremaine said, quickly. "They were men on horses. At least, I *think* they were men. And they were chasing one of those deer-things."

"Like the one we saw last night," Carter added, for Officer Davies's benefit.

"Oh dear." She looked unhappy. "That last one was enough trouble to remove. And we had some very odd calls about it. A professor from some University demanded that we keep it for study. As if we can simply store dead deer like that!"

"Well, he may find another one if he gets here soon," Andrea muttered. "It didn't look like it was going to escape from the hounds."

The police woman shook her head. "I don't know what this is all about," she said. "But I'll have a drive around and see if I can find anything. I'll pop back and let you know later. I just hope I can find one of the hooligans responsible for this."

"I'm not sure you really do want to find them," Andrea said. "Officer Davies, they were... Well, I know this sounds crazy, but they were *dead* people riding those horses."

The police woman smiled back at Andrea as if at a small child. "They'll wish they were dead if I catch them." She nodded, and walked away.

"Some people just won't listen," Carter said sympathetically. "But she seems smart enough and she'll learn. If she's lucky, she'll live through the learning curve."

Andrea sighed. She rather liked Officer Davies, and hoped nothing bad would happen to her. Then she
remembered what she'd been planning on doing. "Mark." She turned and

41

banged on his bedroom door. "Mark, are you okay?"

"I would be if you lot let me get some peace," came the annoyed reply.

"Did you see or hear anything earlier?" Dr. Ballard asked.

"All of you making a deal too much noise. Can't I get any peace to work?"

"Mark, will you come to the door?" his father demanded. "I don't like carrying on a conversation through wood. It's very rude."

"Then you should leave me in peace. Oh, all right. I'm coming!" After a moment, the door was thrown open, and Andrea had her greatest shock of the evening.

Mark was *standing*, using the warped wooden stick they'd dug up as a kind of crutch. He looked pale and sweaty, but he was *standing*.

On his supposedly-dead legs.

Dr. Ballard was as stunned as she, so nobody spoke for a few moments. Andrea just stared as her brother stood, wobbling and uncertain, his weight on the old stick, glaring at them.

"What?" he finally growled. "If this is your idea of a conversation, it's really boring, and I've got better things to do."

"Mark," his father finally said, "you're standing!"

"Yeah, I *did* notice that. Is that all you wanted to say to me?"

"The doctors said it was impossible!" Dr. Ballard protested. "That you'd never walk again!"

"And doctors are always right?" Mark scoffed. "Maybe I should fall down, just to justify your faith in the medical profession?"

"No, of course not, but..." Abruptly, Dr. Ballard laughed. "This is wonderful!"

"Yeah, it's a miracle." Mark scowled. "Can I go back to what I was doing now?"

"We should celebrate or something," Mrs. Tremaine suggested.

"Spare me the cups of tea," Mark begged. "Look this is all very touching, but I'm kind of busy, so if you don't mind, let's call it a night, shall we? I'll still be able to stand in the morning, and then you can make a fuss over me if you like."

"Oh, you must be exhausted, you poor thing!" Mrs. Tremaine

agreed. "We should help you back to your bed – "

"I don't need any help," Mark said curtly. "I'm used to looking after myself. Good night." He closed the door, almost slamming it. Andrea could hear him shuffling away from it.

"That's wonderful, isn't it?" Mrs. Tremaine asked happily. She looked at Dr. Ballard. "Almost a miracle."

Andrea wished she could agree. But there had been something that didn't seem quite right about the whole thing. Mark was still as angry as ever – surely regaining his power to walk should have made him happy? Or was she just being grouchy herself? Shouldn't she be happier for her brother, now that he seemed to be recovering?

The adults went off, chatting happily together about Mark. They seemed to have already forgotten about the Wild Hunt. Andrea, however, felt terrible qualms. Glancing at Carter, she was almost relieved to see that she wasn't alone.

"Am I the only one who finds this recovery a bit suspicious?" Carter asked her. "Let's face it, yesterday Mark was definitely still crippled. And today he's standing up and walking." He shook his head. "And not a faith healer in sight."

"No," Andrea informed him. "I'm... ambivalent about it, too. We see a strange storm, get a visit from corpses hunting an extinct elk and then Mark starts walking... I can't see how they can be connected, but I can't see how they're *not* connected, either. Do you know what I mean?"

"I know exactly what you mean," Carter agreed. "There's something really strange going on in this house, and your brother's smack dab at the center of it."

Andrea had to agree. Somehow, Mark was involved in whatever was happening. But how could he be? And *why*?
And what was really happening? "Life's very strange all of a sudden," she said slowly. "And it began when Mark found that stick on the beach."

"Yeah." Carter scratched at the back of his neck. "He seemed to be so certain *something* was there. Like he'd seen it in a vision or something."

"Given what's happening, maybe he did." Andrea sighed. "Somehow, something's happened to him. He's finding lost sticks and now walking. Carter, I'm happy for him, but it scares me. The doctors were all absolutely certain he'd never walk again. His nerves were destroyed in the crash. There's no way for him to control his legs."

"Maybe the nerves grew back?" Carter suggested doubtfully.

"Overnight?" Andrea shook her head. "No, however he's been cured, it's not by any natural power I can think of."

"Then what sort of power? I'm a realist, and I don't believe in magic."

"I didn't believe in ghosts, either," Andrea said. "Until tonight."

"The Wild Hunt wasn't ghosts," Carter complained. "They left too much damage for that. They were *real* somehow."

"So how do you fit that into *not believe in magic*?" Andrea demanded.

"I don't know – yet. But it has to fit somehow. Science explains everything."

"What about all of those stories you always tell about King Arthur and everything?" Andrea realized she was making fun of him, but she couldn't help it.

"For God's sake, Andrea – they're *stories*. I don't *believe* in them; they're just fun things to tell to the tourists."

"Like me?"

"Of course." He shrugged. "Great tall tales, and there's probably a bit of truth in them somewhere. But nothing more than that. There are no knights, no Round Table, no ghosts and no magic. There's just truth and scientific fact on one side and wild stories and superstition on the other. People only believe in magic because they wish it to be true. It's not how the universe works."

"Right now," Andrea warned him, "I'm almost in the wild stories and superstition camp myself. I can't explain what we've witnessed any other way. And nor can you."

"A time warp of some kind," Carter almost pleaded. "That was your own idea, remember? The elk came out of the past!"

"And what past do you know of where corpses ride horses?" she yelled at him. "Or maybe that's something I missed in History 101?"

"Okay, I have a problem with that part," he agreed defensively.

"But I'm sure it'll all make sense when we find out what's happening."

"I don't want to find out," Andrea told him. "I want it to just *stop*. To leave us alone."

"Where's your sense of adventure?" he chided her.

"My sense of self preservation killed it!" Andrea knew she was getting a little hysterical, but she couldn't help herself. All of her emotions were overwhelming her. "Carter, what's happening *terrifies* me! Somehow something evil is working here. The Hunt, the dead elk, Mark walking..." She shook her head. "I can't take much more."

There was a loud rap on the door beside her and it was all she could do not to shriek. Carter, grim-faced, pulled it open.

Officer Davies was standing there once more. "I drove around the area," she informed them. "And I found another of those bloody deer, dead in the road. This is getting to be quite a nuisance."

"More than that," Andrea told her. "It's getting to be very scary." She shuddered. "You didn't see what was chasing that elk."

"No." The police woman looked abruptly more sympathetic. It made her look younger, and Andrea realized that the woman was only in her early twenties. It was the upswept hair and uniform that made her look older. "Look, love, you've obviously been through a bit of a strain. I think you need to get some sleep. I wish I wasn't on night duty – I'd love to crawl into bed myself."

"I'm too scared to sleep," Andrea replied. "Maybe the Hunt will come back."

"I doubt it," Carter told her. Then he grinned. "Want me to stay with you tonight? I wouldn't mind."

"I'm sure you wouldn't," Andrea said drily. "But I can think of four people who would – our parents and me."

The police woman patted her arm. "If I were you, though, I'd sleep with the light on. It might make you feel better."

"Yeah, I'd look like a child!" Andrea growled.

"That's not what I meant, love," the police woman said. "We all need some comfort at times you know – and you look like you could do with a heap of it right now."

Andrea felt guilty that she had reacted so poorly. The poor

45

woman was just trying to help. "Thanks, Officer Davies."

"Call me Blodwen, love; everybody else does. And we do seem to be seeing a lot of each other these days."

Carter grinned. "You want to take in a movie, then?"

"You're a cheeky little blighter, aren't you?" She didn't look annoyed, though, and she grinned at Andrea. "You'd better keep an eye on your boyfriend."

"He's just a friend," Andrea said quickly.

"Well, keep an eye on your friend, then." Blodwen looked at the sky, now thankfully dark again. "And keep the other one peeled for trouble. I've a strange feeling it's not over yet."

"No," Andrea agreed miserably. "I think it's just beginning..."

Chapter Five

The following morning, Mrs. Tremaine decided to try fixing what she could in the garden. Andrea felt that she really should help out, since the Tremaines had been so good to her family. Gardening was not her favorite occupation, however, though she forced herself. And of course it turned out to be a really beautiful day, the first in ages. There was so much else she would have preferred to do, but obligations had to be met.

Mark didn't feel the same way, naturally. He had turned up, finally, for breakfast, walking with the stick. He had a strong limp, but it was astonishing just that he could walk. This miracle, however, had not changed his sourness, and he'd snipped back at any questions while he ate. Then he informed everyone that he was going to practice walking. He turned down all offers of company, and set off alone, slowly, down the road.

"I'm going to follow him anyway," Carter decided. "He can't be strong enough, really, to walk by himself."

"You're just trying to dodge the work," Andrea accused him, though she was glad that somebody would be watching Mark.

"You bet I am," Carter replied with a grin. With a cheery wave, he left. Andrea shook her head. Boys! Oh well...

She worked hard all morning, helping to salvage what they could of the ruined plants, and filling in clods of grass where the horses had passed. It made her back and knees ache, but at least it gave her time to think. And Mrs. Tremaine insisted on breaking every thirty minutes or so for a cup of tea, which helped, though Andrea was getting quite tired of endless tea. Hadn't anyone heard of coffee in this country?

She couldn't help brooding, however. Something very strange was definitely happening, and it had only begun two days ago. The first week of their stay had been pleasant but uneventful. This had all begun with Mark's odd mood on the beach. But what had provoked that? She was almost ready to

believe that somehow Mark had become possessed. What could possibly have cured his lameness? And how could it be tied into the arrival of the Wild Hunt?

Everyone was talking about this. They had not been the only ones who'd seen the Hunt, it turned out; most of their neighbors had simply stayed indoors, too afraid to come out. They were out in force this morning, though. Several of them stopped by to see Mrs. Tremaine – and, clearly, the damage the Hunt had caused – and to ask questions and to offer their theories. Unsurprisingly, most were connected with the possibility of the End Of The World. The Mayans even got a few mentions, though Andrea couldn't see what they could possibly have to do with any of this. The one thing from all the nonsense that they spoke that intrigued Andrea was that none of them had seen anything like the Hunt before, and they had never even heard of anyone who had. Some of the neighbors had tried to make sense of it the way the Tremaines had – by denying that most of what they had seen had happened. One person was even convinced it had been a motorcycle gang roaring through town that had caused the trouble! But several mentioned the Wild Hunt, and referred to stories that their grandparents had told them when they were young.

Clearly, this was something new – or, more likely, something very old that had started up again. But why? What was the catalyst for all of this? And how did it tie together? No matter how hard she thought, though, Andrea could come to no conclusions.

When it was almost twelve, Mrs. Tremaine decided it was time for her to fix lunch. "Go find those two boys, will you, dear?" she asked Andrea. "I don't imagine that Mark will have managed to get too far, and I suspect that Carter's gone off to play or something. I'm rather worried that Mark might be overdoing things. It's wonderful he's walking again, but he mustn't tire himself out from the excitement."

Andrea thought that Carter was a bit old to be playing anywhere, and that "excitement" was hardly the word she'd have chosen to describe Mark's reaction to his miracle, but she agreed to make a search and be back in half an hour, with or
without them. She set off down the road to the village that they had both taken. The day was still fine, and it actually felt

reasonably warm – the first time since she'd arrived in England. It might actually be almost 70 degrees, instead of the usual, miserable Fifties.

Tintagel was a nice, compact place, centered around the high street, like so many English towns. Here were the shops and the ever-present pubs. Farther out were the hotels and bed and breakfast places. The castle, the town's main attraction, was down by the sea. Nestled around the main part of town were the inevitable housing estates with row after row of virtually identical houses. There wasn't any reason for Mark to have gone there, even if he felt up to it, so he'd have to be somewhere near the center of town. She saw a few people she vaguely recognized from the past week, and they waved hello to her. The locals seemed to be a cheery sort, so she waved back, even when she was unsure who she was greeting. But there was no sign of either boy. Glancing at her watch, she saw that it was about time to head back. With a mental shrug, she did so. Maybe the boys had already returned home, and she'd just missed them. If not, they could fend for themselves.

Andrea was almost back at the Tremaine house when she saw Mark, alone. He was down one of the side streets, and seemed to be intent on something. He was bent over near a stone wall, poking with the walking stick. Andrea called out, and then went closer. Mark, as usual, simply ignored her. When she saw what he was doing, she gasped.

He'd cornered a young cat, trapping it against the stones, and was jabbing savagely at it with the gnarled stick. There was an expression of pleasure on his face each time the terrified cat hissed and clawed at him. The cat had several bloody welts on its body, and it was clearly in a panic.

"Mark!" she snapped. "Stop that!" How could he possibly be so cruel?

"Go away!" he growled, not looking at her. He slammed the stick into the cat again, and it screeched with the pain.

Furious, Andrea grabbed his wrist. "Stop it!"

Mark whirled to glare at her. "Stay out of this!" His face was twisted with fury, and he jerked his wrist from her grip. "This isn't your business."

"Leave the poor thing alone!" she insisted, knocking the stick aside. The cat seized its chance and bolted, a long streak of blood-specked gray.

"Now look what you've done!" Mark whirled angrily on her, raising the stick in the air. He seemed to be able to stand without it now.

"Are you going to hit me now?" she demanded, refusing to back down. "Mark, what's got into you?"

He blinked, as if finally aware of what he'd been doing. He lowered the stick again. "Nothing's gotten into me," he said sullenly. "And you know I wouldn't hit you. You may be bossy and interfering, but you're still my sister."

"Well, thank you for that back-handed compliment." Her concern for him was starting to outweigh her anger over his behavior. "Why were you hurting that poor cat?"

"It annoyed me," he replied curtly. "Look, did you want something other than to interfere with my fun?"

"You call that cruelty *fun*? You were enjoying hurting that animal, weren't you? Mark, that's not like you; normally, you're very gentle. What's gotten into you?"

"There's nothing wrong with me!" he exclaimed. He held out his hands, and turned around. "Look at me – I'm almost whole again. Why can't you just be happy for me?"

"I'm happy that you can walk," she assured him. "But I'm not happy about what else has happened to you. You're getting nastier and more bitter every day."

"Don't you think I have a right to be bitter? I've been confined to that wheelchair for a year of my life. It's enough to make anyone bitter."

"Not like this." Andrea touched her brother's shoulder, but he jerked away. There was no point in arguing with him. "Come on, Mrs. Tremaine has lunch ready now."

"Good, I'm starving." He set off, and Andrea was amazed at how well he was now walking – almost as fast as before his accident. There was no sign of a limp, but he swung
the stick as he marched. It was an amazing improvement since this morning.

Too amazing...

Carter had turned up also to eat. "Mark seemed to be fine," he explained to Andrea, "so I left him to it. He caught me following him, and gave me a mouthful." It sounded all too much like Mark. After they'd eaten, Mark announced that he was going off again, and this time didn't want to be followed.

"Don't worry," Carter assured him, "I'm not coming near you. I hope you fall and break both of your legs."

"I'm more likely to break both of yours." Mark jabbed out with the stick at Carter, who jumped back to avoid being hit. Laughing at his sick humor, Mark stormed off.

Carter stared after him thoughtfully. "Would you like me any less if I beat the stuffing out of your brother?" he asked Andrea.

"Sometimes I'd like to do it myself," she confessed. "He was torturing a poor cat earlier. There's this cruel streak in him that wasn't there before."

"I'd have thought getting his freedom back would have cheered him up," Carter said. "Instead, it seems to have made him nastier. Go figure." He grinned. "Anyway, I've got some gardening to dodge. I'll see you later." He waved and shot off.

Andrea sighed, and went outside to find Mrs. Tremaine. Carter's mother smiled at her sympathetically. "I'm sure you've had your fill of this, love. Why don't you go and have some fun this afternoon?"

"But I can't leave you to do all of the work," Andrea protested.

"Everybody else has," Mrs. Tremaine pointed out. "I think you've done your share. Go and enjoy yourself."

Still feeling a little guilty, Andrea did so. She had no idea where either Carter or Mark had gone, but she didn't need their company to enjoy herself. Instead she went back down to the beach to think. With the waterfall behind her, she walked the cool sands and enjoyed the breeze off the ocean.

This was quite near where Mark had insisted they dig for that silly stick...

She looked up at the castle, and then decided to walk through Merlin's Cave. It was cool and damp and salty inside the cave. As always, there was discarded litter. Some people couldn't see a pristine place without wanting to leave a McDonald's wrapper or soda can, it seemed. Even somewhere as pretty and fascinating as this.

51

There was a faint whisper, and a tickle on the back of her neck. Andrea whirled around, thinking Carter or Mark was trying to play a joke on her, but she was quite alone in the gloom. Puzzled, she continued to spin in a circle, looking for anyone who might be teasing her. She could hear some kids playing on the beach, but there didn't seem to be anyone in here with her. Maybe she was just getting spooked. Considering what was happening, it wasn't too far-fetched a thought. She started on again.

There was a whisper, like the tiny echo of a voice, close by, but sounding far-off. "Who's there?" she asked, softly. Not alarmed, just... wary. Maybe it was some sicko? Everyone had been nice to her in England so far, but there had to be crazies over here, too. Someone who saw a lone, pretty girl in a dark cave and thought he could take advantage of her? But all she would have to do was scream and there were dozens of tourists on the beaches. Nobody would be stupid enough to attack her in such a public place. Would they?

Besides, she didn't exactly feel scared. More... well, expectant. As if something was about to happen, and not something bad. Something... well, just strange, maybe. Uncanny – that was the word for it. Her eyes flickered about, but she could see nothing. Yet she had the clear impression that there was someone or something close to her, so close that she should be able to reach out and touch something. She reached out, but there was only empty air.

Worried, she turned and ran back to the beach. She stopped outside the cave, breathing in short gasps, looking back at the dark entrance. There was nothing there, of course, and back out in the sunshine, she felt foolish. She was letting shadows and imagination mess with her mind. She needed to
get a grip. Undecided, she stood there, looking around. Then she elected to go back to the village, to the warm, friendly, comforting shops. Where there were people doing simple, everyday things and she didn't have to be alone.

She spent an hour or so ambling around. She bought a couple of postcards for friends back in the States and wrote short, silly messages. Then she mailed them, killing more time. Finally, she went back to the house. Mrs. Tremaine had packed in gardening, and was getting dinner ready. Andrea pitched in to help, glad to have something to occupy her mind.

There was a funny feeling about the house, too. It seemed to be centered on Mark's room, and it was a little like the oddness of the cave. Only here it seemed darker, more oppressive, like some giant shadow was hanging over the brightly-lit room. Andrea stood in the doorway, looking in. Mark liked his privacy, and wouldn't be happy if she went into his space. But she could see discarded paper in the waste basket, and she had an urge to see what was on the sheets. She knew she shouldn't, and she also knew that she was going to anyway. In a rush, she darted for the basket, and pulled out the top sheets.

Puzzled, she looked through them. They were all drawings of a tree – an old, warped, leaf-free tree that twisted across the pages. It made no sense at all, since Mark wasn't into botany or even artwork for that matter. The drawings were good, quite detailed but somehow *wrong*. Well, technically, they were very perceptive. It was just that looking at them made her feel uneasy. As if there was something twisted about them in more ways than the obviously physical.

With a guilty start, afraid Mark would return and see her with them, she threw them away again and left his room abruptly. It all meant something, she was sure. The only problem was making any sense out of it all.

The two men came home from work, and her father went upstairs to read a bit until the meal was ready. Carter arrived a little while later, with the unmistakable scent of the local hard cider on his breath. His mother scolded him, but Carter didn't seem too worried by that. "I only had a pint," he protested.

"You're too young for that stuff," his mother complained. Andrea knew that the local cider was quite alcoholic, much more so than back home in the States. "And you're not too big yet that you can't have your backside spanked, you know."

"Let Andrea spank me," Carter suggested. "I might even enjoy it." He waggled his eyebrows at her. "Or maybe I should spank her; *she* might enjoy that!"

"Lay a hand on me," Andrea warned him, "and you'll get it back with one less finger!" He laughed at that.

"You can't talk sense to him after he's had a drink," Mrs. Tremaine advised her. "It's just teenage foolishness, that's all. Don't pay him any mind."

"I shalln't."

It was almost seven now, and still no sign of Mark. Mrs. Tremaine clucked her tongue. "I can't hold dinner any longer," she decided, "or it'll ruin. He'll just have to have his heated up when he comes home. Fetch the others, would you, love?"

There was still no sign of Mark even after dinner was over. Andrea helped with the dishes, and Carter actually volunteered also. He seemed to have recovered from his earlier silliness, and kept looking out of the window. Night had fallen, and stars were starting to appear. Even though the night looked nice, Andrea was chilled; would the Wild Hunt be back tonight?

And where was Mark?

"I think we'd better call the police," Dr. Ballard finally decided.

"Andrea and I could go look for him," Carter suggested. He didn't sound too keen on the idea, though.

Dr. Ballard shook his head. "Given what happened the last two nights, I think you two would be better off staying home. It's the job of the police to look for missing persons, anyway." He headed for the phone to make the call.

Carter gestured for Andrea to come with him, and they went into the hallway together. "I don't much care for your brother sometimes," he confessed. "But I wouldn't like my worst enemy to be out if the Hunt is riding."

Andrea knew what he meant. "Maybe we had better stay home, then," she said. "If we were caught outside..." She didn't have to finish her thought; Carter shivered as visibly as she did.

"Maybe we should barricade the house." Carter sounded like he was only half-joking.

"I don't know," Andrea answered. "We might need to get out in a hurry."

Carter gave her an odd look. "Why do you say that?"

John Peel

"It's... just a feeling," Andrea confessed. "I've been feeling kind of odd all day. Like I'm being watched, or somebody is trying to talk to me or something." She sighed. "It's all so vague... Like you feel after watching a horror movie. Creeped out and expecting something to jump at you from every shadow. It's probably just my imagination."

"You're the least imaginative person I know," Carter told her. Then he grinned. "I mean that in a completely complimentary way, of course!"

That made Andrea smile weakly. There was still this knot of apprehension in her stomach. "Something is going to happen," she predicted. "I *know* it. I just don't know how I know it. It's something to do with the castle..." If only she could shake off the feeling, but it was growing stronger in her. *Something* was drawing close...

It took about ten minutes for the police to respond. Andrea was hardly surprised or unhappy to see it was Blodwen again.

"Don't you get any time off?" Carter asked her, cheekily.

"With you young hooligans in the town?" Blodwen smiled. "I'm pulling extra hours. Very nice for the bank account, let me tell you. Now, do you have a picture of this missing boy? I don't recall ever seeing him with you."

Andrea hurried to get a photo she'd taken a few days back. Mark was in his chair, scowling as usual. Blodwen
raised an eyebrow.

"Well, if he's chair-bound, he should be really easy to spot."

"He's not in his wheelchair anymore," Andrea replied. "He... started walking today."

"Just like that?" Blodwen asked, slowly. "Then he can't have gotten far; his legs must tire easily. Maybe he fell over – did you check the hospital, to see if he'd been brought in?"

"Mum did," Carter said. "She always checks them first; bloodthirsty mind, if you ask me." He frowned. "Hang on – where are my folks? And your Dad?"

Andrea realized that they were alone with Blodwen, which didn't make any sense. Where were the adults? "I'd better check," she said. She went back into the living room, and stopped in the doorway. Her father

55

and Carter's parents were still there. All three were sprawled in chairs, apparently asleep. That was bizarre and for some reason scary. She crossed to her father and shook him.

He grunted, and twisted away from her, but didn't waken.

"Carter!" Andrea cried, alarmed. "Come here!"

He and Blodwen both rushed into the room, and stared at the sleeping adults.

"I can't wake them," Andrea said, a catch in her throat. "What's going on?"

There was a sudden roaring sound, and the house started to shake.

Chapter Six

"What's happening?" Blodwen cried, as the floor rocked beneath their feet. Andrea grabbed the door-frame to steady herself.

"Earthquake?" suggested Carter, staggering across the room to join them. His parents and Dr. Ballard slept on, obviously undisturbed by the event.

"Not an earthquake," Andrea gasped. "I've been in one, and it wasn't like this. We'd better get out of the house. And take them with us. If it gets worse..."

There was no need to speak further. Andrea grabbed her father, while Blodwen and Carter took his parents. It was difficult to keep their feet anyway, but with the dead weights they were carrying, it seemed to take forever to weave their way to the front door and then outside. Andrea's arms were aching, and she felt like throwing up. It was like trying to walk down the deck of a sinking ship. Eventually, Blodwen called a halt, and they lowered their sleeping burdens to the lawn.

"This should be far enough," Blodwen said, breathing heavily. She'd lost her cap somewhere, and her hair was falling down from its usual neatly-pinned bun. "They should be safe here if the walls collapse."

The ground was still shuddering, but it didn't seem quite as bad now they were outside. Andrea groaned, and stretched, trying to overcome the cramping of her muscles. Night was thick about them, and there was no sign of any stars now. She glanced about apprehensively, but there was no sign, either, of the Wild Hunt.

The quaking continued, and then Carter gestured down the road, away from town. "Look!"

Andrea followed his lead, and she saw what had caught his attention. In the road, a strange depression had formed, just as the ground shook. It looked for all the world like a footprint – some six feet across. But there was nothing
visible that could have caused it. A moment later, the ground shook again, and another print appeared, cracking the tarmac and leaving a faint,

smoky haze, some twenty feet closer to them.

"There's something there..." Carter breathed.

"Something *not* there," Blodwen contradicted him. "Something invisible, and it seems to be heading this way."

"Is it after us?" Carter wanted to know.

"No," Andrea said. She couldn't tell why, but she was sure she was right. "It's heading for the castle. And so should we."

Carter gave her a pained look. "Go to the castle? Are you nuts?"

"No." Andrea felt more and more certain that her feeling was correct. "It's where we should go. It's where we're meant to be. Trust me."

Blodwen nodded. "I have this strange feeling that you're right," she agreed. "But I don't know why. Just something drawing me..."

Carter looked from one to the other. "Let's get a grip," he suggested. "There's something invisible stomping through town, and you two *think* we should head for a really exposed spot where we'll have the sea at our backs and no line of retreat?"

"Yes," Andrea and Blodwen said together.

Carter sighed. "Well, okay. I just thought *somebody* should be pointing out how stupid this plan of action is, that's all. So, you want to jog?"

Blodwen gestured at her waiting police car. "I think that's a more logical way to get there."

"So do I," Carter agreed. "I was just afraid that the two of you were throwing logic completely to the winds, that's all." They ran for the car.

There was another quake as the invisible foot slammed down – this time, onto a BMW parked outside a house. The rear end was crushed completely, and the car alarm started screaming. "I wonder how the owner's going to explain *that* on his insurance claim," Carter muttered. "Uh, maybe we
could hurry it up here, before we're the next to play sardines?"

Blodwen had the car started and moving. Andrea was beside her in the front and Carter –staring nervously over his shoulder - in the back. The invisible *whatever* was now about a hundred feet away – about five steps, Andrea realized. Hopefully they would gain ground on it because of the car's speed.

"Can we put on the lights and siren?" Carter asked. "I always wanted to do that."

"And attract who-knows-what attention?" Andrea pointed out. "That invisible giant thing back there might not be the only thing loose tonight..."

Now she'd put her feelings into words, Andrea realized how true that was. The night was dark, but there were flashes of light, low to the ground. Not fireflies, she knew, because fireflies only gave a quick burst every now and then. This flickering was something luminous, lots of them, moving about swiftly, like swift, tiny, glowing birds. She wasn't at all sure that she wanted to know what they were.

And, even with the windows of the car closed, she could feel that there was something stirring the air. There were whisper-like noises in her ears, and invisible fingers touching her and darting away. It was obvious from Blodwen and Carter's reactions that she wasn't the only one being bedeviled.

"Am I the only one who's regretting having seen *The Exorcist*?" Carter asked, swatting at things he couldn't touch. "If either of you starts swivelling their heads, I am so going to be out of here."

"I don't know what's happening," Andrea said. "But it's not all bad..."

"It isn't?" Carter looked incredulous. "Can you tell me what about this whole mess *isn't* bad? Trust me, there's nothing happening right now that makes me feel in the slightest bit happy. *Especially* what we're doing."

Andrea couldn't explain. It was simply something she felt, deep within herself. "There's something good out there,"
she finally said. "Only, it's attracting a lot of evil. The evil is trying to smother it, to stop it from happening..."

"So, maybe we should head in some other direction?" Carter suggested. "And let the good and evil fight it out? Then we can come out when it's all safe again." He seemed to have abandoned his reliance on science and logic right now.

"And what if the evil wins because we do nothing?" asked Blodwen. She shook her head. "I'm a police officer; it's my job to fight evil."

"I'm a student, and it's my job to goof off and to hit on girls," Carter objected. "I really don't think I should be here."

"I'm glad that you are," Andrea said simply, and touched his hand.

Carter looked at her and shifted uncomfortably. "Okay, then, I'll stay. But only on the condition that you understand that, technically, I am now hitting on girls. No other reason..."

Andrea understood that he was scared, and trying to cover up for it with his silly attitude. She felt grateful for his presence, and didn't care what means he used to justify it. She knew that there was something that she had to do, and it would be easier for her to handle it if he was around.

But *what* was she to do? That wasn't at all clear. She simply felt a push, as if there was something she was meant to do, something vitally important. Only the identification of what it was seemed to be missing from her awareness.

It was scary, really, that she was getting these feelings. It wasn't like she was some sort of psychic hot-line girl, who normally got messages from beyond. But now, somehow, there was a non-voice in the back of her mind, calling her toward it. She *felt* that the presence meant her no harm, but how could she be *sure* that this was the case?

She couldn't, she realized. She could only trust that her instincts were right. And pray that if she were wrong, she'd live to regret her mistake.

Blodwen pulled the car to a halt at the top of the slope leading down to the castle. "Let's go," she said, firmly. She pulled the useless pins from her hair and tossed them aside. Andrea saw that the police woman had a mass of black hair that made her look even younger and certainly less official.

They all piled out of the car and started down toward the visitor center. The pathway was always steep, but it seemed tonight like they were heading down the slippery slope to destruction. Fear plucked at her heart, and Andrea had to steel herself to keep going. She noticed sweat on Blodwen's forehead.

"Uh, either of you noticed what's happening ahead?" Carter asked. His voice was squeaky with fear.

Andrea looked at the castle and understood what he meant. The whole island was lit with a pale blue light. Vortexes of luminescence swirled above the area, like dancing winds. It was as if giant fingers were stirring the air, making it glow.

"This is way too *Indiana Jones* for me," Carter muttered. "I don't suppose either of you would listen to a plea to get the hell out of here?"

"No." Andrea was firm in her reply, even thought she desperately wanted to say *yes!* She knew that there was something waiting for them at the castle, though she couldn't say what. She *had* to go through with this.

They had reached the gate, which was locked. Andrea looked at it, annoyed. She hadn't thought about this. She couldn't believe they were being baulked by a simple gate. Then Blodwen managed a weak smile, and took a bunch of keys from her pocket. "I have a key," she explained. "You never know what you'll need on patrol."

There was another quake, as the invisible footprints started catching up with them again. They looked back in time to see Blodwen's car get crushed as something immensely heavy stomped it to a thin film on the road.

"At a rough, guess, another patrol car," Carter muttered. "If we *must* be crazy, could you please hurry it up?"

Blodwen had the gate open, and they hurried across the bridge to the main part of the castle ahead of them. Now the interference became worse. The hands plucking at Andrea started to slash, with sharp, invisible nails. She gave a cry as one attack left a long, bloody welt down her left arm. The other two were being similarly assaulted. They covered their faces as best they could and pressed on. The fingers clutched at her clothing, trying to drag her to a halt, or maybe even just rip them off her body. Fighting, she struggled forward.

The pale blue light was growing more intense as they advanced. It seemed to be seeping from the rocks and the ground, illuminating everything from below. It cast preternatural shadows about them, making Andrea gasp. But, deep inside, she knew that she was doing the right thing, and going the correct way.

There was a flash beside her, and she stared as the shape took form. It was vaguely humanoid, but only about four inches long. It was naked, but unformed, like a slightly melted Barbie doll. And it had wings that beat to keep it in the air. *A fairy?* Right now, that wouldn't surprise her; she was almost beyond shocking.

Then it turned to look at her, and she saw it had a feral snout. With a snarl, it opened its mouth, and showed twin rows of sharp, nasty teeth. It plunged at her, and snapped closed on the back of her right hand.

Andrea screamed, and grabbed the creature with her left hand, ripping it free, and leaving a stinging, bloody gash on her hand. She threw the creature to the ground and then stomped on it. She heard the sound of breaking bones with dull satisfaction.

Then there were more of the things, filling the air about them. They dove in, snapping and tearing, and retreated when they could. Many of them fell victims to blows from the besieged trio, but the stream of them seemed to be endless.

Not far now...

It was a real voice this time, Andrea knew. She could hear it echoing in her mind, even though it hadn't spoken aloud. She glanced at Blodwen, and saw confirmation there that the other woman had heard it also. Swatting the vicious little flying things, they pressed on.

Ahead of them was a low stone wall, one of the relics of the oldest castle. It seemed imbued with a supernatural light, glowing, beckoning to them. This was the place they had to be, Andrea realized. They had reached their goal.

Their attackers seemed to realize it also, for they were going frantic in their assaults now. Andrea had stopped screaming, because she simply could hardly hurt any worse than she already did. Blood was dripping from her hands and face, and she could see that Blodwen and Carter were just as badly off. One of the creatures lunged for her eyes. In panic, Andrea barely managed to swat it aside and then crush it beneath her soggy shoe. The thought of those sharp tiny teeth ripping into her eyeball was terrifying.

Just ahead of her, there was a slight glow, not the pale blue of the stones and earth, but an orange, warm glow. It was small, but irresistible. This was it! This was where she was meant to go! She put out her hand, only to immediately have it bitten. Fighting back the pain and tears, she grabbed for the glowing orange object, and felt her fingers close about it.

A sudden shock went through her, as if she had touched an electrical socket. She gasped, and then jerked back, still holding the object. She could see now that it was some sort of a medallion, made of a very fine metal. In the glow, she couldn't make out what was on the object, but that hardly mattered. She pulled it in close to her body, determined that her attackers would not get to it.

She felt a surge of strength flowing within her. Whatever this medallion was, she was reacting to it somehow. She felt warmth from within rise and flow. Power seemed to be leaching from her and into the medallion. Something within her seemed to be aware of what she was doing, even if she couldn't understand it or name it. She focused her thoughts, her energies, her very life into encouraging the power flood into the object.

Light sprang from between her fingers, spilling out of her clenched fist. The orange glow spread, growing. The evil creatures screeched, as if in fear or pain, and started to pull back. Andrea glanced up, and saw that they desperately wanted to attack, but fear – or something even more powerful - was driving them slowly but firmly backward. Andrea sighed, glad of the relief. There was pain all over her body,
and she collapsed with her back to the stone wall. Blodwen and Carter slumped down beside her. Both of them looked as bad as she felt, with blood trickling from dozens of sharp-toothed wounds.

"I think they've had enough," Carter gasped. "Maybe they don't like the taste of us."

"It's not that," Blodwen said. "Help is on the way, and they can't stand up to it."

"I can't stand up to anything right now," Carter muttered.

There was a crack like thunder, close by. Andrea turned her head slowly – she couldn't move it faster – and saw the ground and rocks seem to split. It was as if a doorway to somewhere beneath the ground was opening up, a crack in the fabric of reality. More of the pleasant, comforting orange light spilled out of it, and then a shape emerged. In the glow, Andrea couldn't make out very much, beyond the fact that it looked vaguely human.

"That was uncommonly well done, my lady," said a deep, masculine voice.

Chapter Seven

Andrea stared at the strange figure, unable to make out any details in the glowing light. Then the man stepped forward, and the gash in reality seemed to stitch itself back together. The light died down, and Andrea could start making out details again.

The man was tall, just over six feet, and very muscular. He had shoulder-length dark hair, but was clean-shaven. His eyes were intense. He wore some sort of leather armor, and a sword slung at his hip. There were leather boots on his feet, and a pair of long leather gloves tucked through his belt. He gave her a smile, then a bow, and took her surprised hand. He then kissed the back of it.

"My lady," he said, "I thank you for your aid."

Andrea found herself blushing, though whether from the kiss or from his respectful manner of address, she wasn't certain. To cover her embarrassment, she held out the medallion. "This is yours, I believe?"

"No, my lady; you worked it, so it is now clearly yours. Wear it about your pretty neck."

"Okay," Carter broke in, stepping forward. "What's going on here? Who the heck are you?"

The man blinked, and then looked from Andrea to Carter and then to Blodwen. "My apologies," he said gently. "I have not introduced myself. I am Ulric, son of Bleoboris, knight of Arthur, the king."

"What?" Carter looked at the man in disbelief. "And where did you escape from?" he asked sarcastically.

"Annwyn."

"Never heard of it. Is it down the coast?"

Ulric shook his head. "No, it is a great deal farther off than that, I fear." He looked around. "The spell I was given is holding off the evil forces, but it will grow fainter soon, and they will return. We must be gone before that happens. Is there a safe place?"

Blodwen sighed. "Right now, I'm not sure anywhere is safe from what's been going on. But I suppose we'd better get away from here for now. It is very exposed."

"Perhaps you would lead the way, my lady?" Ulric suggested.

Blodwen snorted. "I'm not usually called *my lady*," she informed him.

Ulric looked worried. "I am sorry," he apologized. "Do I have your rank incorrect? Please forgive me. Are you higher than a lady?"

"Most people wouldn't think so." Blodwen gestured for everyone to start walking. "Just call me Blodwen, okay?"

"Blodwen?" Ulric considered. "It is a fine name. And what is the name of my lady?" He gestured at Andrea.

"She's Andrea," Blodwen replied. "The surly one is Carter."

Ulric nodded. "He is her servant?" Carter almost choked, and Andrea giggled.

"No, I bloody well am not," Carter snapped. "Though she sometimes acts like I am. What's with you? You act like you don't understand anything."

"I am unfamiliar with your world," Ulric said. "But I must learn swiftly, before the end of all things overtakes us."

Carter shot Andrea a significant look, and twirled his finger in the air beside his temple. "This chap is absolutely cuckoo. I don't know where he came from, but I wish he'd go back and leave us in peace."

"No," Andrea said, firmly. "I'm not sure what's happening, either, but he is the one we came here to meet. I know that." She held up the medallion, and then placed it about her neck. "Somehow, I was called there to free him. Even if I don't know how I did it."

"Indeed you were, Lady Andrea," agreed Ulric. "The spell was placed to bring the most suited to the gateway. You, naturally, were the most suited."

"*Spell*?" Carter shook his head. "I tell you, this guy is nuts."

Andrea sighed. "Look, the Wild Hunt rides the skies, extinct elks roam the night and an invisible giant stomped
Blodwen's car. Why are you now having a problem with accepting the idea that Ulric isn't from this Earth?"

"Because my credulity is overloaded!" Carter growled. "I can only believe in six impossible things before breakfast – or after dinner. I just want something nice and normal to happen again, instead of all of this insanity."

"That will not happen as long as the Outwand is loose," Ulric informed him.

They were making their way up the path to the village now. Andrea could see the flattened police car ahead of them. "We can't drive anywhere in that," she said, puffing slightly.

"You have no horses?" asked Ulric, looking about.

"We don't use horses much these days," Blodwen informed him. "Generally, we prefer cars."

"Cars?" He looked blank.

"He *must* be from another world," Carter muttered.

"How far from the castle should we get?" Blodwen asked the knight.

"A little father yet," he suggested. "That is where the evil ones will commence hunting for us. We need to travel, but first we must talk. There is a great deal I need to know."

"There's a great deal *I* need to know," Blodwen said. "Right, let's head for the closest pub." She glanced at Andrea and Carter. "They'll let you in as long as you're with me. But we're heading there to talk, not to drink." She looked sternly at Carter as she said this; clearly she knew about his taste for the local cider.

They hurried down the main street, which was oddly deserted. The only signs of any activity were the still-smoking prints of the invisible giant in the street. The giant itself seemed to have vanished. Ulric looked curiously around as they walked.

"These are strange buildings," he commented. "And even stranger roads. Don't your horses hurt their hooves on this ground covering?"

"We don't use horses," Andrea reminded him.

Blodwen pushed open the pub door. Normally, a wave of noise from the jukebox would have hit them, along with the
sound of talking, glasses rattling and the smell of cigarettes and beer. Tonight there was only silence. Wasn't there anyone here tonight? They moved inside, worried. The patrons were all there, and all sleeping – some with their heads down on the tables, others where they had fallen to the

ground. The barman was snoring behind the bar. The whole scene was really unsettling.

"Just like our folks," Andrea said. "Why is everyone asleep but us?"

"The Outwand is hunting us, Lady Andrea," Ulric said. "It has no use for these people yet, so it has rendered them unable to interfere."

"Okay, come on." Blodwen led them through to a small room at the back. There were a couple of empty tables there, and she gestured for them all to sit. Andrea felt a little odd sitting in the bar, with people sleeping all around, but Ulric seemed to take it in his stride. "Right," the police woman said firmly. "We all need to know just what is going on here. We can't act sensibly if we're kept in the dark."

"There is a great deal of truth in what you say," Ulric agreed. "So I will attempt to explain what I can, and then you must inform me of what you know." He took a moment to gather his thoughts.

"As I told you, I am Ulric, son of Sir Bleoboris, and knight of Arthur, King of all Britons."

Carter shook his head. "Arthur's just a story people tell," he complained. "He probably never existed."

Ulric gave him a firm look. "Arthur *exists*, because I have seen him with my own eyes. All the surviving knights have seen him, these past thirty years. My father, alas, is growing a little old, else he would have been the one to come back from Annwyn, not I."

Andrea was starting to understand some of this, thanks to having paid attention to her father's researches. "Carter, wait," she said, before he could start arguing again. "Annwyn is the Welsh name for the Underworld, where the dead went. And Sir Bleoboris, according to the stories, was one of the few knights to survive the final battle between King Arthur and Modred."

"But they're just *stories*," Carter protested. "Enhanced to make the tourists happy. They're not history. I should know – I tell them all the time."

"And Annwyn is not a place of the dead, Lady Andrea," Ulric added. "It is a place of the living. But it is not on this world. It is where Arthur was taken, when he was sorely wounded, to rest and recover from his wounds. He sleeps still, until the time of great need, when he shall waken and return to save England."

Even Andrea was having a difficult time accepting this, and this was despite the certainty she felt that Ulric was being completely truthful. "That was over sixteen hundred years ago," she said, softly.

"In this realm, yes," Ulric agreed. "But in Annwyn, time passes more slowly. There it has been but thirty years since the battle. I was born there, some twenty two years ago."

"I guess *some* people do more than sleep there," Carter muttered.

"We have a small castle there," Ulric explained. "The surviving knights who wait to serve their king again live and train there. There are various ladies also, and servants, and also the Lady of the Lake and her attendants."

"How about Merlin?" asked Andrea eagerly. "I always wanted to meet a true magician."

"Alas, Merlin lives no longer. He was tricked and killed by Nimhue, which is part of the story I must relate. We have only lesser magicians these days, who could cast some small spells." He touched the talisman that Andrea wore. "One of their number sent this token through to your world, where the right person could activate it and open the gateway from Annwyn. But it would allow only one person to cross, and I was the one chosen. I was given some small protective spells, to fight back the evil creatures that follow the Outwand. We knew that its creatures would attempt to prevent my crossing."

"You mentioned this... Outwand before," Blodwen said. "What is it, and what does it have to do with all of this craziness?"

"The Outwand is *causing* these demonic manifestations," Ulric replied. "It is the sole cause of all the evil now begun. Lady Andrea mentioned the Wild Hunt riding – that is because the Outwand is breaking the barriers that held their world apart from your world in the past. As to what the wand itself is..." He took a breath.

"Back at the creation of all the worlds, there was a Tree. In the Bible of the Christians, it is known as the tree of the knowledge of good and evil. In the legends of the Northmen, it is called Yggdrasil, the World Tree. I believe that in other cultures, the tree has other names and attributes. But it was and is the first-born of all creation.

"This tree has its roots in the Underworld, its trunk in this world and its branches in the Heavens. By its very body, it holds the three areas of creation both together and apart."

"Together and apart?" Blodwen frowned. "I'm afraid that you've lost me there."

"Together," Ulric explained. "The roots hold firm in the Underworld – Annwyn. This is one world. The trunk passes through this world that you now live in, joining it to Annwyn, and at the same time, it keeps Annwyn and this world from coming together. And then the branches support the skies and the Heavens, keeping them attached to both other worlds, and yet separate."

Carter snorted. "I've got news for you," he said. "There's no tree that does this. Science has explained the origins of our Earth very well, without any mention of trees that grow through the Earth."

Ulric frowned. "I do not know this *science* of which you speak, but I understand your meaning. You see no tree, therefore there is no tree." He shook his head. "It is not that simple. There are... layers of reality. If you take a pile of clothing, then they look like a single entity. But you can lift off a pair of leggings, and they are no longer connected to the others. Where they touched before, they no longer touch. Does this mean that they have changed their nature? No, they are what they were before."

Carter snorted again. "Does anyone have a clue what he's talking about?"

"Yes," Andrea said. "What he means is that it is possible that *both* science and mythology may be right. The Earth might well have coalesced out of primitive star stuff – and, at the same time, the World Tree, in another form of reality, could still hold it together. The one doesn't negate the other."

"As far as I'm concerned, it does," Carter muttered. "Science and superstition don't mix." But he sat back to listen further.

"The Lady Andrea understands my meaning," Ulric agreed. "I am no philosopher, and I am probably explaining this badly –"

"You are," Carter muttered again.

"-- but this is the truth of the matter: the World Tree holds the layers of reality together, and, at the same time, holds them apart, so that they do not intermingle, except in small areas."

"Ghosts, and sightings of monsters," Blodwen said. "Loch Ness, and all that. Overflows from Annwyn or the Heavens..." It did make a kind of sense.

"Now, when men were formed, some men realized the power of this Tree. It could not be reached easily from this world, but one there was who managed to gain access to it. The one you named as Merlin. He was the greatest magician this world or any other has ever known, but even his power could not keep him safe.

"Merlin was a wise and learned man, and deeply skilled in magical arts. But he was, after all, only a man. And he had the passions and blindnesses of any man."

"Why do I have the feeling that here's where the woman comes into this story?" Blodwen asked.

Ulric gave her a radiant smile. "I see that you are a wise and learned woman, Lady Blodwen," he commented. "Yes, indeed, there came a woman. Her named was Nimhue, and she, too, knew magic. And she craved power – Merlin's mantle, to be exact. She was a woman of charm and great beauty. I never met her, of course, but my father did. He told me that any man would have given half a kingdom for her love, perhaps even Arthur himself. So it is of little surprise that Merlin fell for her wiles. Since our Father, Adam, was seduced in the Garden of Eden, women have always been able to have their way with men."

"That sounds rather chauvinistic to me," Blodwen sniffed.

"Lady, it is not," Ulric assured her. "Men think themselves strong, but they willingly become weak for love. It is women in this world who hold the true reins of power, for they can shape men to their will."

Blodwen gave him a funny look. "I take it you don't have a wife or girlfriend in this Annwyn of yours?"

"No, my lady. I am a knight, dedicated to my cause. I have had no time for pleasures."

"I thought not." Blodwen sighed. "And you've probably been around men too long. Well, one day those silly ideas will be knocked out of your head, but I don't suppose this is the time to start, or we'll never hear the end of this story. Go on."

"Nimhue went to Merlin and convinced the great magician to aid her in her quest. She had long known of the World Tree, and she had formulated a plan. If two wands were cut from opposite sides of the trunk, they would be connected to the power of the Tree, and enable the bearer of the wands to draw on the Tree for strength. Merlin should have known better, but he was blinded by his lusts for Nimhue, and readily agreed. Together they cast the spells, and together they cut the two wands.

"And that is when the great evil began. The wands were... I hardly know the words for this... *alive*, for the Tree is alive. They had minds of their own, and their powers could not be simply bent to do the will of the bearer. Instead, the wands sought to twist the wills of whoever held them to do as the wands desired. And the two wands had very different personalities.

"The first wand was named Caliburn, and it was cut from the good side of the Tree. The second wand was named Mara, and was cut from the evil side. But Merlin, then, did not know the wands had their own minds. He thought them
simply tools and nothing more. As a result, Mara was able to enter into his mind and see what it was that Merlin wanted above all. The great magician longed for peace in England, of course – an end to the dynastic squabbles that had caused wars for too long. Caliburn helped with this, showing Arthur to Merlin and enabling him to create the Knights of the Round Table. The code of the knight was introduced, and each man sworn on his honor to uphold the good.

"But, at the same time, Mara was doing its work. It poisoned the good, polluting the work of Caliburn. Mordred was born, Guinevere betrayed Arthur, Lancelot turned traitor, and the last battle was fought. Excalibur was found and almost lost, and Arthur cut down. Everything that Merlin had worked for was turned to nothingness. Merlin himself vanished."

Andrea nodded. "In one story, Nimhue was supposed to have trapped him inside a tree and stolen his powers. Given what you're telling us, that story seems to be likely."

"That may indeed be true; I cannot say." Ulric sighed. "However, Nimhue also vanished, so there is none left to tell their tale. After the great battle, Arthur was taken to the Isle of Annwyn by the Lady of the Lake, and there he rests, recovering from the wounds he received. He lies there still, and will awaken only in the time of England's greatest peril.

"Meanwhile, my father, Bleoboris, and the few remaining knights, agreed to go and wait in Annwyn with their lord. But first, they were supposed to have destroyed Mara, ending its evil forever. One knight, Malacthus, was sent to do this. He was never seen again, but it was always believed that he had succeeded in his quest. Now, however, it has become clear that he did not."

"What do you mean?" asked Blodwen, puzzled. "I've never heard of this wand of yours ever being used again."

"Nor has it," Ulric agreed. "Until now. The outlaw wand has been silent and bided its time, until the right person for it came along."

"This wand..." Andrea asked slowly, afraid she knew the answer. "It's just a little thing, right. Six inches long or so?
You wave it and *hey, presto*?"

Ulric scowled. "No, my lady. I do not know what you mean, but the wand – which we call the outlaw wand or Outwand – is not small. It is of a length to lean upon."

Andrea gave Carter a chilled stare. "It's that stick that Mark found," she said slowly. "That's the Outwand. *He's* got it."

"No, my lady," Ulric said firmly. "*It* has got *him*."

Chapter Eight

Andrea struggled to take all of this in. "This... *Outwand* has taken over Mark?"

"I believe so, my lady," Ulric agreed. "It preys upon those it feels an affinity for. It must have sensed something within your brother that it could exploit."

It was making a strange sort of sense. "His anger," Andrea realized. "He was crippled in an accident. And after he found the stick, he could walk again."

"It must have promised him healing," the knight realized. "That was how it corrupted him."

"Corrupted?" Andrea hated to think that way about Mark.

"The Outwand is evil," Ulric said gently. "It must be affecting your brother."

Andrea remembered the cat. "He's started being cruel," she said softly. "Hurting things..."

"Mara is at work here. We must find your brother, and swiftly."

Carter rolled his eyes. "We were actually thinking of that before you arrived," he pointed out. "The problem is, we don't know what happened to Mark. He's gone walkabout."

Ulric looked very concerned. "This is not simply about one person," he said. "The Outwand is working on what it has always desired – destruction. At the moment, it is planning the destruction of the World Tree itself."

Blodwen scowled. "That doesn't sound very smart. Didn't you say that the wand draws its power *from* the Tree? Won't destroying the Tree cut off its own power?"

"That is one possible result, yes, my lady," agreed Ulric. "The other – which the Outwand is counting upon – is that with the Tree destroyed, all of its power will then be channeled through the Outwand and Caliburn."

"That doesn't sound good," Andrea agreed.

"Worse than it sounds, Lady Andrea," the knight said gravely. "If the World Tree is destroyed, then the words it holds separate will come together. Such a collision of worlds is hardly likely to leave many beings alive."

"Oh, great," Carter muttered. "So now it's the end of the world we're facing? This is all sounding a tad hard to believe." He glared at the knight. "I don't mind six impossible things before breakfast, but this is just too much."

"You yourselves mentioned the presence of the Wild Hunt," Ulric stated. "That is not the only manifestation of the folks of Annwyn in this world. The invisible giant, the fey creatures, the deer that should not exist... All of these manifestations are caused by the unbinding of the strings that hold reality together. And these things will only intensify unless the Outwand can be found and destroyed. If we do not do this, the worlds will come together, and we may well face the destruction of all life as we know it."

Carter sighed. "I'm really thinking it's a shame I'm too young to get drunk. It's bound to make things look better."

Andrea ignored him. "So, we have to find my brother and destroy the wand?"

"Yes, Lady Andrea," agreed Ulric. "And we must do it swiftly. I am certain that the wand has a plan, and that is what your brother is about at this moment."

"That's all very well," Blodwen said. "But we don't know where Mark is, and we don't know what he's doing. Unless you've brought an Evil Detector with you?" She looked at the knight hopefully.

Ulric shook his head. "I am armed with my good sword, and a few decaying spells," he said sadly. "As I mentioned, we have no great magicians left us."

"Which means we have to rely on our wits and luck." Blodwen sighed. "I really hope our luck is good, because I'm rather afraid our brains are in short supply at this moment."

"I have faith in you, my lady," Ulric said simply. "You have a competent air about you."

"Well, that's one of us with faith." Blodwen looked from one to

Outwand

the other. "I'd say that we're all about running on empty as far as ideas are concerned." She glanced at her watch. "Goodness! It's past two already. I think our best
course of action is to get some sleep. We'll all think better when we're rested and with some breakfast in us."

"A wise plan," Ulric approved. "Shall we stay here?"

Andrea looked at the sleeping patrons. "I'd sooner have my own bed," she said. "Can't we go home?"

"I don't see why not," Blodwen agreed. "It's a quick enough walk." She looked Ulric over. "I imagine he can sleep on the couch. Though how we're going to explain him to your folks in the morning..."

"Plus, there may be a clue in Mark's room to show us what he's up to," Andrea said. They headed for the door. "I found some drawings of trees there earlier. He must have been thinking about the World Tree when he drew them."

They walked past the sleeping people in the main bar. Blodwen looked thoughtful. "You said that the Outwand wants to destroy the World Tree," she said to the knight. "How can Mark get to it from this world?"

"I am not completely sure, my lady," Ulric answered. "There are certain places with magical connections, so I assume he could get to it through one of those. But I have no idea which he might choose. And, as I say, I have no magic about myself to open any such doorway we may find."

"Some help you are," Carter muttered ungraciously. Andrea glared at him; his attitude wasn't helping at all. She could empathize a little with him – like her, he was going through major shock here. Discovering that magic existed and was infesting their sane, rational world was bad enough. But he had no underlying faith to fall back upon, except in science – and that was looking very shaky right at this moment. Everything he had believed was true was being shaken and changed, and that couldn't be easy for him. But that was little excuse for his uncharacteristically surly mood.

The night was crisp and dark. Andrea glanced about apprehensively, but the nasty flying creatures seemed to have vanished.

76

Perhaps the remnants of Ulric's magic still held them at bay. Or... She fingered the amulet gently. Perhaps Ulric was right, and somehow she had some kind of magic within herself... Though she didn't feel any different. There
were no globes of light or crackling sparks from her fingertips
as there would be in Hollywood movies. It was hard to believe that there was anything special about her.

Thankfully, there was no sign of the invisible stalking giant.

Which didn't, of course, mean that the night was safe...

The conversation faded away miserably as they started up the road to the Tremaine house. The town appeared to be deserted, though there were plenty of lights on in the houses. There was no sound from TVs, though, and no movement, even of animals. It was like walking through a disaster site. There were the smoking footprints still crushed into the road, each of which they carefully skirted. The whole effect was one of terrible creepiness.

"What's that?" asked Blodwen, suddenly, her head jerking. "I can hear something..."

Andrea couldn't, at first. The police woman's hearing was obviously very sensitive, because a few seconds later, Andrea did hear something. It was a low, keening sound, coming from the night air.

"An owl?" Carter suggested. He sounded more hopeful than confident, though.

"There are no animals stirring this night," Ulric said firmly. "They have better sense than to tempt the powers of evil."

"Better sense than we have, it seems," Carter commented.

"Animals are closer to the powers of nature than civilized man," Ulric replied.

"It sounds like somebody screaming..." Blodwen said. "Perhaps it's somebody hurt?"

"Maybe the Wild Hunt is at it again?" Andrea guessed. "They could have caught another elk and be killing it."

"It is something moving," Ulric said. "The sound draws closer. I do not think it is anyone in pain – at least, not in physical pain. I have never heard a sound like this."

Andrea looked around. The sound *was* getting louder, and with surprising speed. If someone was approaching them, they were moving very, very quickly...

And then she saw it: *it* being the operative word. It looked vaguely like a flying woman, but that was simply because the creature was composed of tatters of substance, glowing yellow in the night. What looked like long hair streamed back from its very vague face. The rest of its body consisted of thin shreds of matter, all flowing in the air as it flew. The face was little more than two large, dark eyes and a wide, tooth-lined mouth. It screamed as it flew, and it was drawing closer to them swiftly.

"What the hell is that?" Carter demanded.

"I suspect *hell* might be the right word," Blodwen said. She looked somewhat pale, and Andrea knew her own face would be the same. There was something terrible about this creature. It might be the way it looked, or the way that scream went right through you. Or, maybe, it was the terror of the prey faced by the predator, because it was quite clear that the thing was heading for them.

"Banshee," Ulric explained, whipping his sword from its sheath. Andrea vaguely had the time to see that the hilt was carved with some intricate dragon design before the gleam of the blade almost blinded her.

The banshee whirled into the attack, diving down at them. Ulric moved forward to block its approach, his sword ready to whirl and slice-and-dice. The creature wasn't stupid, however, and it whipped past him, just out of striking range, before plunging to the attack. It had long, thin fingers, with long, thinner nails. What looked like dried blood had congealed on several nails.

Carter threw himself aside and then yelped as his shoulder hit the garden wall of the house they were beside. Andrea had a second of staring into the tooth-lined mouth before she could get her own shaking body to respond. The wall was only about five feet tall, so she threw herself across it, and down the far side to safety. As she did, she felt the wind of the banshee's passage and heard its scream of frustration as it missed its target. She'd crushed somebody's geraniums in her fall, but she'd apologize later. If there was a later.

The banshee screamed again, as Blodwen threw herself out of its path. Then Blodwen screamed, the long, razor-sharp talons catching her back as she moved just that little bit too slowly. Andrea, looking back, saw the spray of blood as the nails tore through the police woman's jacket and blouse, and then into the flesh below.

Then the creature was past, and Blodwen was lurching to her feet. She'd stopped screaming, but she was definitely injured. Andrea had no idea how badly; the banshee had risen above them, and the scent of blood evidently was driving it crazy for a kill. It howled as it rose to gain height to attack once more. Ulric leaped to place his own body between the monster and Blodwen. Andrea could hear Carter groaning on the far side of the wall. He'd hurt himself when he'd collided with the wall. She glanced upward, and saw the banshee was studying its potential victims. It was hardly likely to go for Ulric and Blodwen; the creature was crazed, but it could recognize the sword as trouble. That meant it would choose either her or Carter, since they were both unarmed.

Andrea glanced around, trying to see something that might give her inspiration to use as a weapon. A spade left out for gardening, or a fork would be wonderful. Naturally, given her luck, the folks who owned this house were the tidy sort. There were a couple of plastic gnomes on toadstools decorating the front lawn, and then a border of geraniums and other plants. Then the house, the side wall, and the garbage cans. Nothing else. Somehow the idea of defending herself by throwing plastic gnomes at a creature of evil didn't seem likely to work.

The banshee had reached the height it needed, and gave another ululating scream as it started to plunge for its intended victim. Her or Carter? Andrea had no option; to stay where she was would be fatal, and if Carter couldn't get away, running from the banshee would only redirect it to him... She waved her hands and screamed, to gain the banshee's attention, and then sprinted for the back wall. If only she could make it think she aimed to clamber over that...

She glanced back as she sprinted, and saw that the thing had indeed focused on her. What a wonderful plan...!
Now it was determined to kill her and not one of the others. She vaguely saw Ulric moving, but had no time to check. As she drew close to the garbage cans, she slowed down, and grabbed at the nearest can. Thank

God that here in England they still used metal cans, not the plastic ones of back home! She wrenched the lid of the closest, and then whirled around, raising it like a shield.

The banshee was moving too fast now to stop, and it was too low to rise. It had been certain it could just sink its fangs and talons into her body, and couldn't pull out.

The thing hit the metal lid with a scream and a clang. The impact sent Andrea reeling, and numbed her whole arm. She lost the lid, which went flying, and she rolled herself across the small patch of lawn and into more plants. Spitting dirt from her mouth and breathing heavily, she looked back.

The banshee, stunned from the blow, had slammed into the garbage cans, scattering old cans, tea bags and scraps of food all over the pathway and lawn. But the thing was strong, and was already recovering. Andrea, her arm still numb and the rest of her body aching, looked wildly around for either of the garbage cans' lids. She couldn't see them. Groaning, she managed to lever herself one-handed back to her feet, but at the same time the banshee, hissing and spitting venomously, was rising up also. It clearly wasn't used to standing on solid ground, and it was still a little disoriented, but it was also concentrating on getting to its prey.

Andrea didn't know what to do now; she'd run out of ideas, and she knew that the seconds of life remaining to her were very short. She whirled to run — if she had the energy to run — and was almost knocked down by a dark shape that rushed past her.

It was Ulric, his sword whirling about his head. The banshee barely had the time to try and block the blow with an upraised arm. Ulric brought the sword down, a crashing, bone-crunching blow. The banshee screamed again as its arm was almost severed, and then the blade bit deep into the throat of the creature. Thin, pale blood sprayed out of the gash, and the noise of the thing was stopped dead. Ulric twisted the blade, freeing it, and whirled it about for a second blow.

It wasn't necessary. The large, dark eyes of the banshee were already glazing over, and it crashed lifeless to the lawn. Ulric regarded the thing suspiciously, and then stooped to wipe the blood from his blade on the things' tatters. Resheathing his sword, he turned to Andrea.

"You are well, my lady?" he asked anxiously.

"Oh, yeah, just dandy," Andrea said. She was simply so relieved to just be alive. Her whole body ached, but it was a good ache – if she'd been killed, she wouldn't be feeling anything now. "How are the others?"

"We must check." Ulric offered her his hand, but she shook her head. She would manage.

She looked down at the dead banshee. "I wonder if it's considered garbage or recyclable?" she mused. Then she turned and limped after Ulric.

The knight paused to check Carter, and then ran on to where Blodwen lay on the pavement, propped on one elbow. He paused, and then simply scooped her up as if she were weightless. By that time, Andrea had reached the front wall of the house. She didn't have the energy to leap it, so she let herself out by the gate.

Carter was staggering to his feet. "I was a lot of help, wasn't I?" he asked, bitterly.

"You hurt yourself," Andrea said. "How's your shoulder?"

"Fine." But he was lying; Andrea could see he held it low, and winced if he tried to move his arm. "Do you think I'll ever play the violin again?"

"Could you play it before?"

"No; I was just hoping to get something positive from this humiliating experience." He looked over as Ulric arrived with Blodwen. "How is she?" He seemed genuinely concerned.

"*She* is reasonably well," Blodwen snapped. There was pain in her eyes, though, and a lot of blood on her clothing. "Though I certainly wouldn't object to either a little medical treatment or else a bottle of something very alcoholic."

Andrea glanced down the road. They were only a few hundred yards from the Tremaine house. "Can you carry her back?" she asked Ulric.

"I can walk," Blodwen growled, trying to get free of his firm grip.

"You will only cause yourself more injury and pain if you struggle," the knight pointed out.

"*Now* you tell me." Blodwen stopped trying to get free. "All right, you can carry me. Just don't get used to it. I don't like being the damsel in distress."

"There is no shame in accepting help when it is offered and needed," Ulric chided her gently.

As fast as they could, they returned to the house. Andrea directed Ulric to take Blodwen to the bathroom and place her carefully on the floor. "Carter, go to my room and see if you can find a loose blouse or something for her to wear." Her own clothing looked in terrible shape. "And both of you close the door as you go." They left, and Andrea looked doubtfully at the police woman. "I'm not really good with blood," Andrea apologized. "But somehow I doubt if there will be any doctors making house-calls tonight in town."

"Do what you can," Blodwen said. "I'll try and avoid screaming too loudly."

Andrea nodded, and prepared the few medical things she was sure of from the family medicine chest in the cupboard. Thank goodness Mrs. Tremaine believed in preparing for emergencies – there were enough supplies to patch up a small crusade here.

Carefully, Andrea removed Blodwen's blood-soaked jacket and then her tattered blouse. Both were absolutely ruined, and Blodwen winced with pain as Andrea peeled the cloth away from the raw wounds. There were three long, deep gashes in the woman's back. Tenderly, Andrea sponged the blood away, applied the dressings and anti-bacterial cream, and then bandaged her up. Throughout, Blodwen managed to stop from yelling, though Andrea knew she had to be hurting quite badly.

"How are you now?" she finally asked, examining her sloppy workmanship.

"A lot better, thanks." Blodwen winced as she turned around. "I'm almost feeling well enough to die now."

"You got the worst of it."

"The bloody banshee got the worst of it. Ulric made certain of that. Speaking of whom, maybe we had better reassure the menfolk that we're okay."

"Just a minute," Andrea said. "I know that those bandages cover a lot, but I doubt Arthur's knights are used to seeing a woman in just a bra wandering around."

That made Blodwen smile. "Yes, they were rather prudish, weren't they?"

Andrea opened the door a crack. "Carter, did you find something?"

"Try this." He handed across one of her blouses. "Boy, you sure like to travel with lots of clothing, don't you?"

"I trust you didn't make a mess in my closet," she grouched. She helped Blodwen into the blouse, which wasn't a bad fit, considering that Blodwen was considerably bustier than Andrea. Then they left the bathroom. Blodwen somehow managed to walk unaided.

Ulric looked at her with concern. "How are you feeling, my lady?"

"How do you *think* I feel?" Blodwen complained. "Bloody awful, of course. But I'll recover. I just need a good night's sleep."

"You can have my room," Andrea offered. Then she shook her head. "Climbing the stairs might be too much for your back. Take Mark's room instead."

"I hope you don't mind if I wish he doesn't come back tonight?" asked Blodwen. "It might be his fantasy to find a woman in his bed, but I don't feel too cooperative right now."

"He won't be back," Andrea said with certainty. "The Outwand has him, and it's up to something... I suspect he's off plotting somewhere."

"There's a pleasant thought," Carter muttered. "Well, I doubt if the precinct will be expecting you to report back tonight, so maybe you'd better get started on resting." He ran a hand through his untidy hair. "Come to think of it, maybe we all should." He glanced at Ulric. "How does the couch sound to you?"

"Anywhere I can lay my head," the knight answered. "I bid both of you ladies a good night."

Andrea walked with Blodwen to Mark's room. "Will you be okay?"

"Sure." Blodwen managed a tight smile. "Compared to the time I broke my leg skiing, this is nothing. See you in the morning."

Andrea went upstairs to her own room. She kicked off her filthy shoes, and wished she had the energy to take a bath. But the bed looked far too appealing to resist right now. Taking off her jeans and T-shirt, she stumbled forward and was asleep almost instantly.

Chapter Nine

In the morning, Andrea felt much better after a long soak in the bathtub. With her hair still wet, she went downstairs for breakfast. She ached, but she'd felt worse than this after sports at school. But she couldn't ignore the pain in her heart as well. Mark was missing, evil was afoot and the world gravely threatened if everything that Ulric had told them was true.

Much to her surprise, the kitchen was packed, but everyone seemed to be in good spirits. Mrs. Tremaine was organizing a mess of breakfast, assisted by a none-too-willing Carter. Blodwen, looking pale but determined, was downing cup after cup of strong, sweet tea. Andrea's father and Mr. Tremaine were deep in discussion with Ulric over an Ordinance Survey map spread across the kitchen table which was by now liberally sprinkled with toast crumbs.

"What's up?" Carter asked her. "Used up all of the hot water, and finally decided to make an appearance?"

"Somebody got out the wrong side of bed this morning," Andrea commented, grabbing a slice of toast and a few aromatic pieces of bacon to make a hasty sandwich.

"We're being left out," Carter warned her, nodding at the table. "Adults only."

Andrea felt a pang at the thought that she was to be excluded from whatever came next. It didn't seem fair! But, knowing adults, it was all too likely. "It's too dangerous..." was the probable reason. She glared at the table, where the three men and Blodwen were hunched over the map. "They can't mean to just dump us here," she complained.

Ulric looked up, and smiled. "Lady Andrea!" he exclaimed, leaping to his feet. "My apologies. Please, have my seat."

Andrea grinned at Carter. "I guess it's just you being left out..." She took Ulric's seat. "Sorry, I *really* needed a bath... Have I missed much?"

"Your learned father has had several excellent thoughts," Ulric

informed her. Dr. Ballard looked pleased
with the compliment, and cleared his throat.

"I've been listening to Ulric's fascinating account of what's happening," he said. If the idea of an Arthurian knight turning up on the living room couch overnight had bothered him at all, he seemed to have worked it out. "It fits quite well into the mythology, and I may be able to help out with a few suggestions. From what I understand, this Mara, the Outwand, seeks to destroy the World Tree." He shook his head in amazement. "You know, when I studied all of this, I always thought it was nothing more than some nice stories. I never expected it to have any practical applications."

Andrea was amazed. "You believe his story, then?" She would have bet anything her father would have laughed himself stupid when he heard the tale that Ulric had spun the previous night.

"Oh, yes. Sir Ulric is clearly quite earnest, and what with Blodwen's details, and what little we could get out of Carter, I think the whole story makes sense. Well, in a way, that is. It is, of course, quite, quite fantastic – but fascinating."

"And urgent," Andrea added. "If Ulric is right, then the whole world must be in danger."

"Yes, right," her father agreed. "Anyway, the most important thing right now is to locate Mark and the Outwand."

"He could be anywhere," Carter objected. He'd come over to stand behind Andrea's chair, and handed her a cup of tea, which she took gratefully.

"Well, that's the point – he couldn't be just *anywhere*." Dr. Ballard looked rather smug. "The Outwand has to get him into contact with the World Tree, which means Mark will need an access point of some kind to get there. There are not many places where such an overlap occurs, and I think that there are only two that are logical choices. You see, it must be a place with its roots in the Arthurian legends, and that leaves us just those two probably sites. I think we can ignore Camelot – South Cadbury." He stabbed his finger down on the map. "It's not really a site of power, just the place where Arthur's capital
lay. Nothing much extraordinary is associated with the site. So we're left

with either Stonehenge or Glastonbury."

Ulric frowned. "I know neither names," he confessed. "But they may have changed over the centuries."

"Of course." Dr. Ballard was right in his element here. "Stonehenge would probably be known to you as the Giant's March. The great stones that Merlin is supposed to have brought here from overseas."

Ulric smiled. "So that story is still around?" He shook his head. "Then I can eliminate that as a possibility. Merlin was a great magician, but he was also a greater liar. He laid claim to many things that were not true, in an attempt to enhance his reputation. The Giant's March was there long before Merlin ever appeared. My father told me the old goat made up some story about finding and fighting a dragon and using the stones to keep it buried under the earth. It's amazing what some people will believe."

"Yes, well, quite. Then that leaves us Glastonbury," Andrea's father said decisively. He stabbed the map again, close to South Cadbury. "That is the site of the Isle of Avalon."

"Ah!" Ulric nodded. "That is indeed a likely place for the Outwand to go. Avalon is where Arthur slumbers, and is, as you say, a place of great power."

"Wait a minute," Andrea objected. "What about right here in Tintagel? We know this is a place of power, and it *is* where the Outwand was hidden."

"And because it is where the Outwand was hidden that this cannot be its goal," Ulric replied. "It is a place of power, true, but not a place to access the World Tree. If it was, the wand would never have been hidden here in the first place. I believe your father has the right of it."

Dr. Ballard looked pleased again. "There is also another point to consider," he said. "There is an ancient abbey there, where the bodies of Arthur and Guinevere are supposed to have been discovered buried."

Ulric snorted. "It seems as though Merlin's legacy of lies lives on; since Arthur sleeps, his grave could not be found."

Andrea's father shrugged. "It was probably just a marketing ploy by the medieval monks to boost visits to the abbey," he agreed. "They were in dire need of cash flow at the time of the supposed discovery. But the association is there. And then there's the Christmas Thorn..."

"The what?" Mr. Tremaine looked blank.

"According to legend," Dr. Ballard explained, "Joseph of Arimathea came to England about 60 AD, and brought with him the Holy Grail, the cup that Jesus used during the last supper. The Grail became the questing object of Arthur's knights. Joseph was supposed to have landed at Weary-all Hill in Glastonbury, and then stuck his staff into the ground. It promptly sprouted as a thorn bush, and it is said to flower once a year at Christmas. Now, in light of what's happened, I would suggest in fact that it is highly likely the Thorn is actually Caliburn, the good wand."

"That makes excellent sense," agreed Ulric. "The whereabouts of Caliburn are unknown to any of us, but it is hardly likely it will be found far from a place of power."

"And if it's true that it is the Christmas Thorn," Blodwen broke in, "then surely that means it should be able to give us help against the Outwand."

Ulric beamed at her. "That, too, makes excellent sense, my lady. I can see that I have excellent allies here."

"So," Andrea said slowly, "this means we have a plan, right? We go to Glastonbury, cut ourselves some wands from the Christmas Thorn – if we can do that without getting arrested as vandals – and then try and find Mark there?"

"That's about it," her father agreed.

"Maybe I'm just being a pessimist," she muttered, "but why does that sound too simple?"

"Probably because you haven't heard everything yet," Blodwen replied. "There is, in fact, a major problem facing us. We don't have transport."

"Oh, right," Andrea said slowly. "Your car got flattened last night." She looked at Mr. Tremaine. "Did yours get stomped too? Or are you just having battery problems?"

"No," he answered. "And it's not just my car that has trouble starting – it's everyone's."

Andrea frowned. "I don't understand."

"Nor do I, Lady Andrea," Ulric said. "But it seems that none of these horseless chariots will move of their own volition any longer."

"It's not just cars," her father said. "It's anything electromagnetic. The TV won't work – just static. The same goes for the radio. I've heard that all aircraft have been grounded, though it's hard to know if that's true or not, since there's no telephones working, either."

Andrea blinked, puzzled. "I don't get it."

"Some sort of electromagnetic pulse," Blodwen offered. "It's scrambling anything that would use electrical power. I don't know where it's come from, but I'd be willing to bet the Outwand has a lot to do with it."

"Oh." Andrea thought for a moment. "So there are no cars, planes or trains running?"

"Well, at least not in this immediate vicinity," her father replied. "Perhaps farther out, but there's no way of knowing. No way of communicating. The rest of the world could be carrying on as normal and we wouldn't know. But I suspect that's not the case."

Things were not improving. "So how do we get to Glastonbury?" she asked. "Walk?"

"It does rather look that way," Blodwen said, sighing. "Oh, well, it will be good for the figure, I suppose."

Andrea looked at the map. "How far is it?"

"About ninety miles," her father said apologetically.

"Bloody hell," Carter muttered. "I don't need *that* much exercise..."

"That would take us about five days," Andrea pointed out. She glanced at Ulric. "Do you think we *have* five days? These manifestations seem to be getting stronger."

Ulric shook his head. "I would say no more than two or three days are left to us at most."

"In which case, there's only one way to get there faster that I can think of," Andrea said. "We ride."

"A horse!" Ulric said happily, catching onto her thought.

Andrea winced; she'd tried riding only once, and her

backside had been sore for a week. And she'd dreaded falling off if the animal moved faster than a slow pace. "No, I was thinking something a little more modern than that," she confessed. "Bicycles. Though maybe you'd be better on a horse. Somehow or other, the idea of a knight on a bike does seem a bit ludicrous..."

"It does indeed," Blodwen agreed. "Now all we need to decide is how many of us are going. Ulric and I, of course. But we can't take too many, as it will slow us down."

"My lady!" Ulric said, alarmed. "Are you sure you will be able to travel? You were sorely wounded this past night..."

"I'll be fine," said Blodwen, firmly. "And while you might be an authority figure in Annwyn, in Glastonbury they'll just take you for another kook. Trust me, there are plenty of them there. But as a police officer, I'll be taken quite seriously." Then she grinned. "As long as I don't try and explain what we're doing, or why we're doing it!"

"Won't you get in trouble with the station here in town, love?" Mrs. Tremaine asked her. "Absent without leave, or whatever they call it in the police force?"

"She does have a point," Andrea's father agreed. "I should think they'll be wanting every officer to work extra duty in the circumstances."

"I think I can get around the sergeant," Blodwen said, grinning. "He owes me a few favors and I've got a mountain of holiday time due me."

"I have to go," Andrea said firmly.

"It's too dangerous," both Blodwen and her father said, almost in unison.

"Stuff and nonsense," Andrea said. "It's just as dangerous staying here. We've already had the Wild Hunt, invisible giants, swarms of evil bees and a banshee. I doubt it's going to get any better until the Outwand is dealt with." She held the medallion up that she'd found the previous night. "And I think I have every right to be a part of this."

"The Lady Andrea is quite correct," Ulric agreed, which surprised Andrea. She'd have bet he'd have wanted her to stay behind and sew something, or do something else
equally lady-like. "The powers of good have chosen her for one of their

champions, and she must accompany us. The fact that she can use the medallion – which requires a grasp of magic – proves that. There can be no argument that she must be one of us."

Dr. Ballad and Blodwen looked like they both wanted to argue about it anyway, but there was something in the firm set to Ulric's jaw that dissuaded them. He was clearly used to being in authority.

"In that case," Carter said, "I go, too. I've been in this from the start, and I'm not going to sit it out now. Besides, somebody's going to have try to talk Andrea out of doing anything daft."

Andrea smiled warmly at him; she'd hoped he'd volunteer, but hadn't wished to ask him. Though she could have done without his insult, which was typical of the way he treated her.

"And I have to go also," Dr. Ballard decided. "After all, I'm the only one of us who knows all of the stories. You need me for my knowledge." He looked slightly uncomfortable. "I only hope I can still ride a bicycle. It's been a few years since I tried..."

"Right," Blodwen decided. "I can get us all bikes from the police yard. This does fall under the vague outline of police work we're doing. And I suppose for Ulric, I could talk to the riding stables. They'd lend us a horse if I asked them, I'm sure."

"Especially if I pay," Dr. Ballard sighed. "Now, what about provisions? Should we bring some along, or buy them as we go? And lodging for the night? We won't be able to cycle the whole way in one day."

"Let's play that by ear," Blodwen decided. "I suspect that if we start planning too much, things won't work out anything like we expect anyway."

"Well," said Mrs. Tremaine, "I suppose that leaves us here to keep an eye on the home front, just in case Mark should turn up. Well, I never did care much for travel anyway. And without a houseful of people to feed, I might be able to get my garden tidied."

"Good old Mum," Carter said. "The world may be coming to an end, but you want your garden neat if it happens."

"Let's get started," Dr. Ballard suggested, hastily. "We've a long way to go, and I suspect we'll need quite a few stops along the way. Sore backsides, and all that..."

That turned out to be quite prophetic. Blodwen had no problems getting them all bicycles, and even Dr. Ballard proved to be reasonably good on his. Ulric viewed the contraption with a mixture of amusement and dismay and definitely decided he'd stick to horseback. Again, Blodwen's connections helped. Ulric found a fine mare that he seemed to strike up an empathy with, and the two of them had to restrain themselves lest they lose the cyclists. Who *did* need to stop fairly often, thanks to them all not being used to that mode of transportation.

Carter sighed at their third halt. "Am I the only one who finds the idea of peddling off on a bike to save the world slightly ludicrous?"

"No," Andrea's father answered, passing over bottled water that Mrs. Tremaine had packed for them. "But if it works, don't knock it. It's better than walking." He rubbed his behind. "At least, in some ways. Why are bicycle saddles always so hard?"

Andrea knew just what he meant, but had no intention of rubbing her own aching muscles in public. She looked at Blodwen sympathetically. "How are you feeling?"

"Not too bad." The police woman stretched slightly and winced. "At least the pain in my posterior is taking my attention from the pain in my back."

The only one of them not sore was, of course, Ulric. He was an excellent rider, and obviously did it all of the time. He seemed to be impatient to be moving, but was too polite to say anything. Andrea couldn't help admiring him. He was handsome, brave, dedicated and charming – quite a killer combination in a man.

Andrea suddenly realized that Carter was glaring at her. She blinked and looked away from Ulric. "What?"

"Nothing." He slammed the half-finished water back into his pack, and slung it over his shoulder. "Maybe we should be going again?'

And so it went, for the remainder of the day. They passed through several small towns, all of whom had the same problem with electrical interference. They were asked constantly for news, but had no intention of causing themselves any problems by talking about the quest they were on. They simply pretended to be on a bicycle tour, and moved on. Of course, it was rather difficult to explain Ulric, so they simply didn't bother; it didn't matter much what people thought anyway. He did get some odd looks, but nobody really asked questions. They probably didn't want to know the answer anyway.

Andrea knew that the English had a reputation for being laid-back and accepting of almost anything, but she was rather surprised that there was no real panic underway. People seemed to be accepting the loss of their cars and TVs without much anger or angst. Nobody knew what was going on, but they just seemed to take it as if it was an everyday thing. It was difficult to ask about manifestations of evil without sounding crazy, but it seemed that most of those had been limited to very close to Tintagel. People in the other towns certainly weren't talking about magical attacks or anything.

"The attacks are probably limited to places of power," Dr. Ballard decided. "So we may be safe from any further assaults until we get nearer to Glastonbury."

"Do you think we'll be attacked there?" Carter asked.

"There is every chance of it," Ulric said. "The Outwand is a thing of great power; I am certain it knows we move against it. It is not likely that we will be allowed to proceed without interference. " That was a sobering thought.

They made good time, since there was almost no other traffic on the road. What there was consisted of other bicyclists mostly, though they did see a few riders. They seemed to be happily taking the chance to ride their horses without worrying about being hit by speeding cars. There were stalled cars to skirt from time to time, as well as parked trucks. A couple of them had been broken into – the locals were obviously not all averse to looting.

They bypassed Exeter, and then hit the M5 motorway. Since no cars, buses or trucks were moving, it was a long, empty roadway, and they made good time.

Sunset was still about an hour off when Ulric decided to call a halt for the evening. They were close to Taunton, but the general feeling was that it might be a mistake to get caught in a town for the night.

"The forces of evil will be more focused there," Ulric explained.

"Where there are more people for them to prey on. And I do not know if this town is sited on a place of power. Many are, as the power drew people together to found the towns. It is best not to take the chance."

"You think it's going to be bad tonight?" Andrea asked him.

"The Outwand will be growing stronger with each passing day. You saw how the forces of evil increased over only two nights. With nightfall, its powers increase. Tonight will manifest darker evil than we have yet seen."

"Oh, wonderful," Carter muttered. "Just what I need to hear to ensure a good night's sleep."

"We'd better post a lookout, then," Blodwen suggested. "Just in case."

"An excellent idea, my lady," Ulric agreed. "I would also suggest that we leave the road and camp out in one of the fields. It will be rough, but for one night, I am certain we can all endure it."

"Wonderful," Carter complained. "We'll be overrun by bugs..."

"Sooner them than ghosts," Blodwen said cheerfully.

Andrea wasn't so sure. The idea of lying on the ground wasn't exactly appealing. She hated insects, and could just imagine them crawling all over her while she tried to sleep, getting into her clothing, and scurrying across her skin... She shuddered at the thought.

"I shall find us some supper," Ulric announced. "These snacks of yours are fine to stave off hunger, but they are not
what heroes need to make them strong. Make you a fire while I am gone." He rode away.

Carter sighed. "I really hope he's not aiming to kill somebody's cow. I mean, I love a good steak, but that could get us all into trouble."

"I think he knows what he's doing," Andrea said.

"Oh, yes. Mr. Perfect, that's him."

Andrea glared at him. "What is *wrong* with you?" she demanded. "You've been in a lousy mood all day."

"There's nothing wrong with me," Carter growled. "I just *love* being sore all over, scared stupid and riding off on a quest to face God-knows-what. I should do it more often."

Mr. Ballard laid a hand on Andrea's shoulder. "Let him alone," he suggested. "He's a teenager, and teens are always moody."

"*I'm* not," she protested.

Her father raised an eyebrow. "Want to bet? Anyway, Ulric wants a fire, and I don't think Blodwen should be carrying firewood with her back problems. Will the two moody teens help me?"

Feeling annoyed, Andrea did as he asked. Blodwen found a small site for them to use, in a meadow, with trees for cover in case it rained in the night. Carter helped her to make a fireplace by gathering stones from a collapsed wall. They didn't want to start a wild blaze, after all. It was one thing to face magic, another to try and stop a wildfire. Andrea and her father collected fallen branches from the copse of trees. She wasn't surprised to discover that Blodwen had a cigarette lighter – even though she didn't smoke - and she soon had a small fire going.

They were feeding larger sticks into it, building it to a respectable size, when Ulric returned. Slung across the horse in front of him was the body of a stag. Andrea felt sad when she looked at the handsome beast's dead eyes.

"Supper," Ulric said, cheerily. "Venison!" He dropped the carcass to the ground, and then tethered his steed to one of the trees on a long rein, so that it could browse for food. The knight then bent over the stag.

"I don't have to watch this, do I?" Andrea asked, anxiously. She was hungry enough to actually eat the meat, but she really had no intention of helping to butcher it.

"No, of course not, my lady." He glanced at Carter, who also looked a trifle pale. "Perhaps you could take her for a short walk?" Ulric suggested. It was a very thoughtful way of excusing them both.

"Sure." Carter grabbed Andrea's hand. "Come on, let's see if there's any fresh water around here. We're probably all just about out." He led her off hastily, as Ulric unsheathed a long knife.

"Thanks," Andrea muttered, as they hurried away.

"No problem," Carter replied. "It's nice to know that I can do *something* at least."

Andrea frowned. "What is wrong with you?"

"I feel so bloody useless," Carter complained. He gestured back savagely. "Superman back there is doing *everything*."

"He's been trained to do this sort of thing," Andrea pointed out. "You haven't. There's no reason to feel inferior."

"I *don't* feel inferior!" Carter snapped. Then he sighed. "Okay, yes, I guess I do. He's just so darned good at everything! I feel useless."

"You're not useless," Andrea replied, realizing his pride had been bruised.

"No? Name one thing I've done today!"

"Looked after me," she replied.

"Like you <u>need</u> looking after. And like you wouldn't prefer to be with *him*."

Andrea suddenly realized what was really bothering the young man. "You're *jealous!*" she exclaimed, blushing. "You think I've got a crush on him, or something?"

"Haven't you?" he asked, angrily. "I've seen how you look at him! Most girls want a knight in shining armor to come to their rescue, and you've actually *got* one. Okay, technically it's leather armor, but you get the point."

"I do *not* get the point!" Andrea snapped. "And you don't know anything, that's for sure. You haven't seen how I look at him, because I *don't* look at him. Well, not in the way
you seem to think I'm looking at him, anyway."

"Oh, right." Carter rolled his eyes.

"I'm getting very annoyed with you," she informed him. "Don't you start accusing me of anything! And, anyway, what business is it of yours *who* I look at in any kind of way?"

"None of my business at all," Carter agreed.

"Then stay out of things," Andrea suggested.

"I shall."

"Fine." She turned her back on him, trying to rein in her anger. How *dare* he say such things about her? She wasn't flirting with Ulric. Okay, he was handsome, courageous, and genteel, but so what? That didn't mean she was falling for him, did it? Her face was flushed, half in anger, half in embarrassment. "Aren't we supposed to be looking for water?"

"So, what's stopping you?" Carter complained. "Let's look."

Silently, they walked on.

Chapter Ten

By the time Andrea and Carter returned – in a thick silence – the butchering had been done, and the cooking of thick steaks over the fire had begun. Andrea had no idea what had happened to the rest of the stag, and didn't really want to ask in case someone told her.

Her father grinned at her. "A most unusual supper," he said. "Venison steaks, potato chips and bottled water." He shook his heads. "And there certainly shouldn't be any stags like the one Ulric killed around here."

"It is a crossover from Annwyn," the knight explained. "Anything living from Annwyn can pass over – as I did – if there is sufficient magic, and then live here in this world. The dead... Well, they can pass over also, but it's harder for them to sustain themselves. But as the power of the Outwand grows, so will the power of other evil things. The dead cannot endure in your world yet – but their time will come."

"Well, that's made sure *I* won't sleep tonight," Carter muttered.

"And it's why we need a watchperson," Blodwen said firmly. "There are five of us, so it'll be less than two hours each. That should make it endurable."

"Two hours each, assuming nothing happens," Andrea pointed out. "If anything comes for us, we'll be awake the whole night..."

That wasn't a cheery thought, naturally, and they all sat about in silence, waiting for the steaks to cook. When they were done, Blodwen had penknives for them all – except Ulric, who it turned out had a perfectly fine knife inside his tunic – and they used large, flat leaves as plates. The meat was a little rare, but Andrea wasn't complaining. It was food, and they were all likely to need the energy later on. She and Carter had accidentally stumbled upon a stream earlier, so once they'd finished eating, they all went down to clean off sticky fingers and penknives.

By then, night had started to fall. Stars were appearing, and Andrea felt a chill. Was it just the wind? She couldn't tell. Maybe it was nothing more than nerves. The others all seemed to feel it, though. There

John Peel

was little chatting, just a short planning session for the travels of the following day. Dr. Ballard hoped they would reach Glastonbury by mid-day, but Andrea thought that might be a trifle optimistic. After this, though, they all fell silent, and by mutual consent it was bed-time.

Blodwen had the first watch, and Carter was to follow her, then Andrea, her father and finally Ulric. Those not on watch used their backpacks as pillows and settled down on the ground, trying to make themselves as comfortable as possible. Andrea was still highly nervous about bugs, but after a while calmed down when none seemed to be terribly interested in crawling into either her clothing or her ears. She fell asleep fairly soon after this.

A hand on her shoulder shocked her awake. Blinking, she looked into Carter's worried face. "Time for my watch already?" she asked.

"No," he said softly. "Time for trouble. Stay quiet, and help me wake the others."

Andrea sat up and saw what he was referring to: there was a green glow on the horizon, and the sound of horses' hooves. This was getting to be all-too-familiar.

The Wild Hunt was out.

Andrea quickly woke Blodwen, and then her father, while Carter roused Ulric. Silently, they gathered together, eyes straining to see what would happen.

They could hear the baying of the hounds by now, and the thunder of the horses' hooves was getting louder as they drew closer.

"Will they pass us by, do you think?" Dr. Ballard asked softly.

"We can pray that they will," Ulric answered. "If they do not..." He touched his sword. "I will give a good account of myself, and try to protect you all."

"There's an awful lot of them, and only one of you," Carter pointed out. "You'll never manage it."

"I will do what I can," Ulric vowed simply. "You are not warriors, and your best course would be to flee if they target us."

The idea of running away didn't suit Andrea, no matter how sensible it might be. Besides, she very much doubted that any of them – all city-folk and clumsy in the country – could successfully elude trained

99

huntsmen.

They huddled together, watching the growth of the light, and listening as the sound of the hounds and horses drew closer. Andrea was praying that the Hunt would simply pass them by – go after another of the stags that Ulric had caught, maybe – when the baying of the hounds grew more frantic.

"I fear they have come across the scent of the slaughtered stag," Ulric said softly. "With luck, they will go to where I buried the offal."

"And without luck?" Carter asked. Ulric didn't answer, because there was really no need for it. They all knew the answer to that.

Andrea waited, her breathing shallow and fast, her heart pounding. The Hunt had passed them by twice – was three times too much to ask? The minutes dragged on, and they could all hear the snarling of the dogs. They were not far away.

And then one of the monsters appeared from the trees, about thirty feet away. Huge, shaggy and staring at them, it stood. Then it gave a single bark. That was obviously the signal for the rest, for more and more of the monster dogs slipped out of the darkness of the woods to stand and stare at the small party. Andrea hardly dared breathe; they had been seen, and that could only mean trouble.

Snarling, the animals lunged forward. Andrea felt herself panic, just thinking about those huge canine teeth ripping into her body, but she forced the scream that wanted to escape to stay trapped within her shaking body. Ulric drew his sword, and stood, waiting, his face grim.

Then the dogs stopped, some ten feet away. Instead of attacking, they formed a closed circle about the party. There
was no way now for any of them to retreat, as Ulric had suggested. They were quite trapped. The dogs were showing intelligence, which was disquieting. Their eyes burned as they watched their victims warily.

The first rider appeared at the edge of the trees. He was tall, brooding, and his body was falling apart. But there was still enough of him left for him to wield a sword and to glare from eyeless sockets at Andrea and her friends. One by one, in silence, the Hunt assembled. Each man was injured, some horribly mutilated, but they all seemed to be oblivious to the pain they had to be feeling. Each of them was armed – swords, maces, axes, or spears – and each of them focused their grim, undead eyes on the small party.

Slowly, they advanced, clearly ready for an attack. Andrea swallowed; what did they have in mind? Carter had said that if the Wild Hunt looked at you, you were condemned to join them for all of eternity, riding with them. The legends didn't say whether they hacked you to death first before you joined them. Were they doomed now, cursed to ride as part of this pack forever? There was no way she wanted to be a part of this, but she had no idea how they might get out of this.

Nor, it seemed, did anyone else. Blodwen was next to her, trying to be brave. But it was awfully difficult to get any confidence from holding a penknife whilst facing these hounds and the riders, and the police woman was shaking slightly. Andrea briefly wished that British police officers carried guns like their American counterparts. Carter looked like he wanted to vomit, and Dr. Ballard was pale and shaking. Only Ulric seemed to be firm, but he was the only one of them who really stood a chance, anyway. He'd been trained to fight, and they hadn't. She imagined this must be almost normal for him.

Then the riders gave a great cry, and waved their weapons as they charged. The dogs in their path melted aside to allow them through. Ulric moved forward, his sword raised to fight. Andrea couldn't be sure in all the commotion how many hunters there were, but there had to be thirty or more.

There was no way on Earth Ulric or any of them could survive this.

She could see the decaying hands raise their weapons, ready to strike, maim and kill; there was blood-lust in the eyes of those who still had eyes. (How could the other riders see without eyes? Why was she worrying about inconsequential details when she was about to die?) The hounds were snarling, ready to leap in after the riders to finish any who survived the blows.

Andrea gave in and screamed. Maybe it wasn't cool, but she'd worry about that later. She just wanted to run, but she knew it was pointless. If she was going to be cut down, she'd face the monster that did it and not take a blow to the back.

The sound of a horn somehow broke through all of the howling and barking. Andrea dropped, as the horsemen thundered at them.

To her shock, the horses simply leapt the party. There were no swords whistling down, nor blows of any kind. Andrea rolled on the ground, and looked back.

The hunters reined in their horses and took up station beyond the circle of waiting hounds. Then, patiently, they simply stared at the terrified party, clearly waiting for something to happen.

"What's going on?" Blodwen demanded frantically.

"I do not know," Ulric answered. He was leaning on his sword, his own hooded eyes studying their would-be attackers. "Why did they call off the assault?"

"Have they called it off?" Carter asked. His voice was breaking slightly, showing the strain he was under. "Or is this just a ploy to scare us?"

"Why would they bother?" Blodwen asked. "I think they can see how scared we are already. If they haven't killed us, they must have a reason for it."

"Well, we're not safe yet," Dr. Ballard cautioned. "They still have us surrounded, and don't seem to be inclined to allow us to escape."

"But why?" asked Andrea. She finally had her voice back. It was shaky, but she was astonished to still be alive to speak.

"I think *that's* why," Carter said, pointing back toward the woods.

A final rider emerged from the trees. This one was quite unlike the hunters, however. Even at this distance, he looked to be huge. He was well-proportioned, and his body was whole, not crumbling into decay like the riders. He wore leather armor not unlike Ulric's, and on his head he had a helm crowned with a massive pair of stag's antlers. He rode forward slowly, and Andrea could see that he had a horn swinging from his saddle. He was the one who had sounded the signal, then. But who – or what – was he?

Dr. Ballard looked excited and terrified at the same time. "It's Herne the Hunter," he said, breathlessly.

"Who?" asked Carter.

"Herne the Hunter, one of the old gods of England," Andrea's father explained. "He is the leader of the Wild Hunt, absolute monarch of whatever he passes through. His word is law in both this world and the next."

"So he's the guy we complain to about these dogs?" Carter asked, trying to joke.

Dr. Ballard shook his head. "You don't want to get him mad at you."

"I think he's already pretty pissed at us if he's sent his men to hunt us down," Carter pointed out.

"They're not hunting us," Blodwen said quietly. "They're making certain we don't get away."

"Had Herne wanted us dead," Ulric stated, "then we should all have our throats torn out by now."

"There's a cheery thought," Andrea murmured. "So, why aren't we dead?"

"Because their lord wishes us alive – at least for now," Ulric answered.

Andrea watched Herne's slow, stately approach. The closer he got, the larger he appeared to be. By the time he reigned in his horse, Andrea could see that Herne was almost eight feet tall, but he was so well-proportioned his true size
wasn't apparent until you got a crick in your neck looking up at him. Herne studied them for a moment, and then removed his helm. Andrea didn't even want to think how much it had to weigh, with those huge horns on it, but the Hunter handled it as if it weighed nothing.

Now they could see his face – it was aging, but not old, with a long, black beard and deep-set, piercing black eyes that studied them all. Andrea shuddered as his gaze passed across her. Nobody dared to speak before Herne finally opened his mouth.

"So, you are the foolhardy folks who are on the quest for the Outwand?"

Ulric stepped forward. "We are, my lord," he said, bowing slightly.

"I don't give you good odds, then." His dark glance swept across them once more. "A woman, a scholar, a girl, a boy not even old enough to shave – and then you, sir knight." He shook his head. "If you are what the stability of the worlds rest upon, then we are indeed in serious trouble."

Carter had been stung by the comment, and stepped forward recklessly. "Yes, well, we're the only ones willing to do it," he snapped. "Unless you're volunteering to help?"

Herne stared at him until Carter paled and backed away. Then the Hunter swung down from his steed, and walked through the circle of his hounds to join them. "That I cannot do," he said flatly. "My realm is confined to that of Annwyn for the moment, and I am forbidden the Earth – normally. But with the barriers breaking down, my men and I have been freed to ride the night again, as we once did in the past." He looked off into the distance – more of time than space. "It is a joy to be free to ride the night winds again, and to feel the greater joy of the hunt once more in this realm of the living."

"Then you're from Annwyn and alive," Blodwen exclaimed. "You *could* help us. You can stay here in the day."

"Woman," Herne rumbled, "you do not know what you are saying. *I* am alive, yes. So are my hounds and horses." He gestured. "But my followers are not. If I stay here past
dawn, they will crumble into the dust they ought to be, and from which only my power holds them. And if I stay, then they must, too, for they are my followers, their destiny tied to mine. I must return, then, to Annwyn before the night is over."

"So you're not going to help us?" Carter asked.

Herne glared him into silence again. "I have already helped you," the Hunter replied. "You are still alive, are you not? Normally any humans my men find would be slaughtered and then join our band."

Andrea swallowed. She had a feeling that Herne's decision might still be rescinded if he was annoyed. "You wouldn't really want us, would you? I mean, you said it yourself – a woman, a boy, a girl and a scholar..."

Herne grunted. It might have been a sound of amusement. "You and the woman might serve to keep my men... entertained. They do not have many diversions." Andrea shivered at that thought. "But you are both scrawny, and would not please too many of them." Abruptly, he grinned, showing pointed teeth. "Besides, I have a mind to allow you to live."

"I don't want to sound ungrateful," Dr. Ballard said, "but why would you do that? Go against your own men and their nature, I mean."

"Because the Outwand threatens me and them as much as it does you and your world," Herne answered. "It wishes to bring the worlds together, to merge the realms. *I* rule where I dwell, but if the worlds collide, then what will be left for me to reign over? Chaos, nothingness... And it is always remotely possible that even I myself might not survive such a catastrophe. No, I, as much as you, wish the Outwand destroyed."

"And that means what?" asked Blodwen. "You already said you couldn't help us."

"I said nothing of the kind!" Herne roared. Andrea paled, afraid he'd been provoked. Blodwen stepped back, pale. "I only said that neither my men nor I can accompany you on this quest. If you think that is all the help I could offer
you, woman, you insult me! You think me so weak and powerless?"

Blodwen swallowed. "I didn't mean to upset you. But what can you do for us, then?"

Herne snapped his fingers, and one of the hounds padded toward them. "First you need a reliable guard for your backs. This is Caldera, chief of my hounds. Like you, he is alive, and he can survive the coming of the day. He will accompany you, and will guide you on your way."

Carter stared at the creature with definite worry. "Uh... is he tame?"

"Tame? Of course he's not *tame*," Herne growled. "He wouldn't be much use if he were. But he will do as I command, and I order him to look after you. Which of you is he to follow?"

There was a sudden silence, and then Andrea screwed up her courage. Normally she liked dogs – as long as they were of a reasonable size and friendly. This was neither. It was huge and shaggy, like a prehistoric mountain that could move. But she felt that it was up to her to do this. "Me, I guess." She stepped forward.

"You have courage, girl," Herne said, and there was almost gentleness in his tone. "Allow Caldera to take your scent."

Nervously, Andrea stepped forward again. The hound padded forward, and she almost ran back. It was huge enough that its face could look directly into hers. It had startlingly blue eyes, almost human-looking, and she could sense a ferocious intelligence behind them. Slowly, she raised her hand, more than half-expecting a set of monstrous teeth to rip it from her wrist. "Good boy."

Caldera glowered at her, sniffing carefully. It growled in the back of its huge throat. It didn't sound happy being referred to as a "good boy".

"You will follow her," Herne ordered sternly. "And guard her. Whatever she tells you, treat it as my command." He stooped to glare into the dog's eyes. "You may be with them, but you still answer to me, don't forget."

Summoning all of her courage, Andrea stepped forward, trying to act as if she had confidence. "Come on, boy," she said, and stroked at the back of its head. He looked at her, and then trotted along to where the rest of the group was watching. Slowly, it walked about the group, evidently sizing them up and getting their scent.

"Right," Herne said, "that's the start of it. You are, I take it, heading for the Isle of Glass?"

"Glastonbury, right," agreed Dr. Ballard, trying not to look like he was watching Caldera as the hound prowled around them.

"Well, you have some sense, then." He sighed, a deep, booming sound. "That is where the Outwand is heading. Unlike you feeble humans, I can sense it. There is very little time left to you. Perhaps one day, certainly no more than two. I can feel the worlds coming closer together. This will grow worse the nearer you draw to the Isle. If you can last until tomorrow night, I will return then and fight alongside you. If you cannot, I will promise to avenge your deaths – immediately before my own."

"*There's* a cheery thought," Carter complained.

"My men grow impatient," Herne informed them. Andrea couldn't sense this, but she assumed Herne knew his followers well. "We must be going – we have to take prey before dawn. It is one of the rules of our existence. Now you are no longer it, we shall have to hunt swiftly." He grasped the reins of his horse and vaulted lightly into the saddle, despite his massive size. Using both hands, he raised his helm and slipped it over his head. "Good fortune be with you all," he called out.

Whirling his horse about, he took up the great horn again and blew a single blast. As one, the hounds – except Caldera – whirled and flowed about the party. The Wild Hunt gave a chorus of cries. Herne touched his heels to his steed's flank, and the mighty horse bounded away. In savage beauty, the rest of the riders and hounds followed after him. In seconds, they had vanished into the trees, leaving only their pallid glow to illuminate their path.

Carter turned to the others. "I don't know about the rest of you," he said, "but I'm going to have real trouble sleeping after that..."

Chapter Eleven

To Andrea's surprise, she managed to fall back asleep after the visit. Caldera curled up beside her, his large, expressive eyes watching everything around them. Despite his huge size, large teeth and aggressive nature she felt somehow very safe. She *knew* that nothing evil would get to her without having to face the hound first and she couldn't imagine anything that would be able to get past it. The others, by unspoken consent, took one look at the dog and decided that no further guard was necessary.

She awoke to the scent of more venison roasting. She rolled over, a little stiff from sleeping on the ground and the cycling she'd done the previous day, and came face to face with the huge hound. He was staring down at her. She almost had a heart attack, looking up into that massive face. Then Caldera blinked, and fell back asleep. Andrea started breathing again.

She shuffled to her feet, wishing for a nice, steamy shower about now. No chance of that, of course. She knew she must be horribly disheveled, but, thankfully, there were no mirrors around to confirm the fact. She really didn't want to know what she must look like right now. And having to wear the same clothes she'd slept in...! Ugh. Grabbing her backpack, she rummaged around for her hairbrush and attacked the grass-filled tangle in the hopes of restoring some semblance of a decent appearance.

Ulric nodded politely to her from his position by the fire. It was low now, but he had a haunch of the dead stag over it, roasting. Andrea's stomach rumbled from the scent of the fresh meat. When she gave up trying to do any more with her hair, she excused herself and went off into the woods. Afterward, she washed her hands and face in the small stream they'd found. She looked up from the stream to see Caldera watching her. He was clearly taking his duty of guarding her very seriously. She went to him and scratched him behind his head. For all of his size and scary ferocity, he was still a dog, and he enjoyed the attention. They walked back to the camp together, her hand resting on his neck, to find everyone else was up now and eating.

Ulric gestured to a portion set aside for her, and then the wreckage of the stag's leg. Caldera didn't need a second invitation; he snatched up the meaty bone and hurried off about ten feet to flop down and devour everything he could. Loud crunching noises indicated that it included the bone itself. Andrea gratefully took her share and ate it with her penknife.

After breakfast, they all washed and refilled their water bottles. Caldera took a long, long drink from the stream, and they all moved back to the bicycles and Ulric's horse.

"I'm not looking forward to getting back on," Andrea confessed, eyeing her own.

"Maybe you should ride that dog you were given?" Carter suggested. "He's almost as big as Ulric's horse." Caldera growled, and Carter quietly went back to getting his bike ready. How intelligent was this dog? Could he understand words?

Blodwen grinned at Andrea. "I'd say he's taken to you, even if he isn't tame. The dog, I mean, of course, and not Carter." She winked. "Anyway, the only thing with the bike is to get on it and refuse to give in. Though I'd love to rest my backside, too."

"Not that much farther to go," Dr. Ballard assured them. "If we make good time, we'll be there by lunch." He sighed. "And maybe we'll find a pub that's open. I could do with a pint to steady my nerves."

"Dream on." Blodwen got on her bicycle, and the others followed suit. They set off back to the M5 again, Caldera loping along quite easily beside Andrea.

The morning went well to begin with, and they managed to keep up a steady, ground-eating rhythm. Once again, there was virtually nobody on the road. There were a few stalled cars left abandoned, so it was clear that the electrical interference was still in effect, and that the results were wide-spread and not limited to the Tintagel area. They bypassed Taunton, though they stopped to look over at the town. Smoke was rising from the center.

"What's going on there?" Carter wondered.

"Trouble," Dr. Ballard said. "It's probably just a normal fire, and not rioting, but when fire engines can't move... And all of the pumps to supply the hoses are electrical... In this day and age, I don't think bucket-chains of people would make much impact on a good blaze."

Andrea seized upon one thing her father had said. "Rioting?" she echoed. "You think that's happening?"

"I hope to God not," he replied. "But it's why I'm steering clear of the major towns. It's been a couple of days without power now, and the food in fridges and shops has got to be going off. Without trucks to bring in fresh, people are going to start realizing that they'd better stockpile cans. And then other people are going to start panicking. There will be demands for camping equipment, bottled water, all that sort of stuff. Anything that can operate without electrical power. And there won't be enough of it to go around."

Blodwen nodded. "If this goes on much longer, everything is going to break down, even if the worlds don't come together and kill people. Trust me, a little privation can cause a lot of otherwise nice folks to become quite nasty."

"Great." Andrea had images of food riots flash through her mind, and of gangs hunting anyone who had something that they didn't... "Just what we need, another reason to hurry up and save the world."

"I don't think it would hurt us to move along," her father said. "It's just a short ride now to the A361, and we'll take that through the countryside. Hopefully, it will be easy going. That meets the A39, and that takes us into Glastonbury."

"As long as there's no trouble along the way," Carter muttered.

They set off again, and found the turn-off just ahead. This new road wasn't as broad and straight as the motorway, but it was still almost empty. The few people they did see were either on bicycles too, or on foot. None of them came near the little party – probably because of Caldera, Andrea
realized. The dog was certainly very intimidating.

After a short while, they came to the little village of Ourton. It was one of those nice English country towns that Andrea normally loved, with a mixture of the pleasingly modern and the hopelessly ancient. Generally, they were friendly little places where people would gossip in the stores and greet everyone with a smile.

Not today. The place looked almost deserted. As they cycled down the main street, Andrea looked around. There was sometimes movement behind curtained windows, but nobody came out to greet them, or even to shoo them away.

"They're frightened," Blodwen said. "No news, no contact with the outside world, no way of knowing what's happening."

"You'd think they'd want to question us, then," Carter said.

"They just want us gone," Ulric observed. "They have no reason to trust us, or to believe anything that we tell them. Besides, your shadow dog probably scares them."

"He scares *me*," Carter muttered.

It was worrying how quickly people could get so frightened. And they didn't even know about the Outwand! Imagine how much more scared they would be if they knew how close to destruction the world was... Andrea shuddered. It all seemed to be so much to place on the shoulders of five people and one oversized dog...

They rode on. A short while outside of town, they saw their first local. It was an elderly woman who looked as if she was about to have a nervous breakdown.

"Help me!" she screamed, rushing from a small cottage garden to block the road.

Ulric, ever chivalrous, reined in his steed. "What is it, mother?"

"It's my husband!" the woman screamed. "He's dead!"

Andrea felt horribly sorry for the woman. To have her husband die on her, like this, atop everything else that had happened to her! No wonder she was in such a state.

"I'm afraid there's not a lot we can do," Blodwen said gently.

"Except, perhaps bury him," Ulric offered.

The woman looked at him as if he were mad. "He's already *been* buried!" she yelled. "Ten years ago, now."

Uh-oh... Was this woman crazy? "Then what's the problem?" Andrea asked, feeling chilled.

"He's *back* again, and pestering me terribly..." The woman gestured toward the house with a shaking hand.

Now she looked, Andrea could see what the woman meant. Thin and uncertain in the bright daylight, she could just make out the outline and vague form of a man. He was pacing up and down, muttering to himself. *A ghost...* she realized, shuddering.

"For him to be abroad and it not yet night, the walls between the worlds must be collapsing swiftly," Ulric muttered. "Annwyn has been breached, and the dead are walking by daylight."

"We'd better get a move on, then," Blodwen said firmly. "Before things get any worse." She looked at the woman. "Be brave," she suggested. "We're doing what we can to remedy the situation."

Yeah, right... Andrea thought. The woman was still having hysterics, but there was nothing more they could do for her. The dead were walking, and Andrea realized that was probably just the tip of the iceberg. If the worlds were so close to colliding, then other, nastier things were almost certain to be on the move.

They were out in the country again when Caldera abruptly growled. His hackles rose – a scary enough sight on its own – and he suddenly plunged from the road, through a hedge and Andrea heard a snarl, a scream, and something getting crunched, very loudly. The scream cut off, and a moment later, Caldera rejoined them, licking his lips.

"I hope that was just a rabbit he was after," Carter said.

"I doubt it; he was acting to protect us." Andrea shuddered. "I don't want to know what it was he caught." *And ate*, she added to herself.

"The worlds are drawing ever closer," Ulric warned. "It could have been any creature from any realm. There will be more."

Toward lunchtime, they reached Street, the largest town close to Glastonbury. Dr. Ballard was clearly hoping for his pint of ale, but he was going to be out of luck. The town was absolutely deserted, at least of real life.

A party of some kind of savage warriors was loose in the streets, howling, and attacking anything in sight. The fact that they couldn't touch anything didn't seem to be bothering them. They had short swords made of bronze that they used to hack at their intended targets – and which passed through them without harm. Sunlight shone through the bodies of the men.

"More ghosts," Blodwen said. "It's surprising how used to them I'm getting. I don't even feel like screaming any more."

"Right," agreed Dr. Ballard. "They're just pains." He walked through two of the fighting men, who looked annoyed at not being able to carve him up. "Maybe we should stop here and look for lunch before we go the rest of the way. I for one will be able to fight the forces of evil better if I'm not starving."

"There is sense in that," Ulric agreed. He glanced around. "Is there some inn we can buy a meal?"

"I should think so." Dr. Ballard peddled on, looking for the nearest pub. He swung around a corner, and came to a sudden halt. "Uh, I think we should retreat..."

"More ghosts?" asked Carter, scornfully. "They're not really a problem... yet. And a few days ago, I would never have imagined I could say that with a straight face."

If it had been ghosts, Carter would have been correct. They were too diffuse in the daylight to cause problems. But it was no ghost that Andrea's father had stumbled across. Caldera started to growl again, this time really low and menacingly, which put Andrea on the alert. As they drew up beside her father, she could see why both man and hound were so upset.

It was a dragon, crouched in the street, eating something that had once been alive – whether human or not, Andrea couldn't see and didn't want to know. The beast was about forty feet long, with a massive body, small head and a long tail that ended in two vicious spikes. If it hadn't been for the unmistakable shape of the snout, and the vague scent of fire and smoke about it, she might have thought she was looking at a dinosaur. Thankfully, the monster seemed to be intent upon its grisly feast, and just looked up as if to assure itself that the intruders had no intention of stealing its meal.

Carter glanced at Ulric. "Uh, I hope there's nothing in your knightly code that says you've got to kill any dragon you come across?"

"I think the best course of action here is for us to slowly retreat,"

Outwand

Ulric replied. "If we were to fight this creature, some of us would undoubtedly be injured."

"Some of us would undoubtedly be frigging *killed*," Carter snapped.

Slowly, they backed away; even Caldera seemed happier with the decision. Then they took an alternative route.

"Now we know why the place is deserted," Dr. Ballard said. "If there are more creatures like that on the loose, this has to be a very dangerous area."

Blodwen nodded, and then she gestured. "There's a pub."

"Excellent." Dr. Ballard led the way, pulling over. He tried the door, which was unlocked. "Anyone home?" he called, but there was no reply.

"I think they must have fled when the dragon turned up," Carter said. "Which, if you think about it, isn't a bad idea."

"We need food and drink," Blodwen said practically. "Let's see if anything has been left behind."

Surprisingly, quite a lot had been. There was evidence that the exodus had been quite abrupt, with overturned drinks on the tables, and half-eaten food. Someone had taken the time to empty the cash register, but not bothered to close it again.

They helped themselves to cold meat pies, potato chips and bottles of mineral water and slightly warm soda. Dr. Ballard found a stash of bottled beer, and brought along a six-pack. He looked at the open cash register guiltily.

"We really ought to pay for this stuff," he said. "But it seems pointless if the money is just to be stolen anyway."

Blodwen touched his arm gently. "Let's just consider this requisitioning supplies, shall we?" she suggested. Dr. Ballard considered this and then nodded.

They headed out of the building, and cycled out of town. They had lunch in the countryside, their destination in view. Caldera didn't seem to care for their choice of lunch, which was probably all for the good. He'd have eaten at least a dozen pies without really noticing it if he'd wanted to. Instead, he set off alone, hunting for game.

114

"That hill there," Dr. Ballard said, gesturing at the mound ahead of them, "is the Tor." Since the land around was fairly level, the Tor stuck up quite visibly. There was a jagged building on its top. "The ruins of St. Michael's Chapel," Andrea's father explained. "The rest of the church was demolished in an earthquake."

"That's where we're heading?" asked Blodwen, finishing her pie.

"Eventually, I suspect so," Dr. Ballard agreed. "First, though, we have to go to the abbey, which is in the main portion of town. There we will check out the Christmas Thorn and see if anyone can give us information. We're drawing closer to where the Outwand must be, though, so I suspect that the danger is going to increase from here."

"As if we weren't all nervous enough before," Carter said with a sigh. "Well, it looks like we're all done for now. I don't think we can put this off any longer, can we?"

"Not if we expect *any longer* to keep on going," Blodwen agreed. "Let's go take on the forces of evil."

They packed their mess away, and then clambered back onto their bikes and horse. Caldera had returned and fell in beside Andrea. He had a tense look about his body, as if he was preparing for trouble. She couldn't blame him. What lay
before them was bound to be at the least very unpleasant and dangerous.

It might well even be fatal...

Caldera abruptly growled, and the hackles on the back of his neck rose. His lips curled back, exposing his immense teeth. The growling was from deep within, an ominous rumbling.

"Something's bothering the hound of the Baskervilles," Carter muttered. When Caldera glared at him, he added: "That's a compliment, okay?"

Then Andrea heard it. Close by, there was the low, keening sound of -

"Wolves!" Ulric breathed.

Chapter Twelve

"There aren't any wolves in England," Dr. Ballard said, automatically. Then, realizing what he had said, added: "Normally."

"As if anything is normal these days," Carter muttered. He was looking around them. "It would be too much to hope that this isn't connected with us, I imagine?"

"It is the work of the Outwand," Ulric said firmly. "And there is more to it than merely wolves." He gestured ahead of them.

It was starting to snow.

"I know English weather is bad," Andrea muttered. "But this is ridiculous."

The snow was starting to come down quite heavily now. At any other time it might have looked picturesque and charming, but the chill that shook her had nothing to do with the weather. There was already an inch or so on the ground.

"This is designed to hamper us," Dr. Ballard said. "It's going to make cycling difficult."

"More than that, I suspect," Ulric offered. "We could simply ride on through this with little ill effect. But it can be no coincidence that there are wolves abroad where they should not be."

"It's an attack," Blodwen said, bluntly. "We'd best be ready for it." Caldera growled, clearly agreeing with her. He *did* seem to understand English. This was one very smart dog.

The sky was getting dark and heavy with the snow clouds that were flying in. The flakes falling were large, the size of quarters, and the snow was getting thicker. Another wolf howled, this time from a slightly different direction.

"How many do you think there are?" Andrea asked, nervously. Generally she liked wolves, admiring their spirit and the way they formed family packs. She always loved seeing them in zoos. She had a strong feeling, however, that these would not be anything like regular wolves and that she would not enjoy seeing *these* beasts.

"I remember hearing that wolves never attack people," Carter said, nervously. "Or is that just another of those Internet rumors?"

"Normally that's true," Blodwyn replied. "There are no authenticated accounts of wolves attacking people. But these aren't normal times, and I strongly doubt what's out there are normal wolves."

"I'm starting to regret not bringing a few firearms," Andrea's father muttered. "Though would they be any use against the supernatural?"

"I'd think a good rifle could bring down even the most supernatural of creatures," Carter replied. "And I'd certainly be feeling a lot braver if we had a few of them." He glanced at Ulric and Blodwen; the knight had drawn his sword and was standing at the alert, his eyes flickering back and forth, while the police woman had a large knife she'd produced from somewhere. "No offense, but a couple of blades won't do us a whole lot of good if there's a pack of them."

"We shall not fall easily," Ulric vowed. "But I do agree that we are woefully unprepared for this assault."

The snow was now ankle-deep, and there was a strange half-light on the landscape. It felt rather surreal, especially since twenty feet back the way they had come from it still looked like summer. "Why don't we just back out of here?" Andrea suggested. "It's bright and warm back there."

"If we retreat now, we may be too late to stop the Outwand," Ulric replied. "We are likely being offered a way out – the Outwand wants us dead, but perhaps your brother still possesses some of his own will and is offering us a chance to survive." He managed a small smile. "That is a good sign, at least – he is not completely possessed by its evil."

"But the longer we wait, the less true that's likely to be," Andrea said sadly. "If we're to save him – as well as ourselves and the rest of the human race, I guess retreat is out of the question." She rubbed Caldera's neck, feeling comfort from this contact. "I think we must continue onward, come what may." The huge dog gave a growl that was clearly meant to mark agreement. To her surprise, the dog prodded gently at her with his nose. She realized it was trying to reassure her.

"Good boy," she murmured.

Unable to ride their bicycles in the snow, they pushed them as best they could. Ulric led his steed with one hands on the reins, the other holding his sword at the alert.

There was a quick burst of wolves baying back and forth. Andrea thought she could detect at least four separate animals, but it was hard to be certain. She peered ahead of them, but visibility was now only about twenty feet. Beyond that everything was blurred by the falling snow. Andrea wiped at her face and shivered; she wasn't dressed for this kind of weather – none of them were.

There was definitely movement ahead of them. Caldera's hackles rose and he glowed, low and deep in his throat. She could feel his muscles tensing, and he was sniffing at the air, seeking the scent of his foes. There was a vague shadow to the left and then the huge hell-hound leapt into the whiteness.

"To me," Ulric said urgently, his sword up and ready. "We must stay together. If the wolves attack, they will go for anyone alone." His horse shied behind him, shivering, clearly scenting predators. He spoke some words in a low, soft tone to it, and the animal calmed a little.

Andrea let her bike fall, as did the others. They moved closer to Ulric, leaving him room to swing his sword if need arose. There was still nothing to see beyond vague, shifting shadows and the feathery puffs of their own breathing. Andrea was shivering, as much from fear as from the cold. Not knowing what was out there in this white nothingness was scarier than seeing something attacking.

Maybe.

There was a sudden burst of snarling and the sound of ferocious fighting. It couldn't be more than twenty feet away, judging from the level of the sound, but Andrea could see nothing. Then a shape came flying at them, slamming into the ground about five feet from her and sliding in a spray of blood-red snow. It was a wolf, its throat ripped out, pumping out its last flicker of life where it came to a rest virtually at their feet. They all shied back, even Ulric, as the blood flowed into the virgin snow.

"That's some dog you've got," Carter muttered.

Then there was definitely something moving toward them from

the white gloom. Four – no, five – shapes, low and lean, snarling in the back of their throats. Andrea could start making out the individual shapes as the wolves closed in. They were large animals, the size of small ponies, all gray and shaggy, with eyes that seemed to burn. They were certainly not any animal born of the Earth she knew. Maybe they were from Annwyn, perhaps from some other place. Whatever they were, they didn't belong here. They slunk forward, obviously picking out targets. She wished she had a weapon of some sort, but only Ulric and Blodwen were armed, though she saw that her father – rather bravely and ludicrously – was wielding his bicycle's tire pump like a club. She doubted it would do much good, but she wished she'd thought of grabbing the one from her own bike. No matter how ineffective it would be, it was better than facing a murderous attack unarmed.

As one, the five wolves moved and then sprang. Andrea had a split-second of sheer terror as she saw the one that had targeted her fly through the air, teeth bared, dripping saliva, eyes burning with murderous hatred, paws and claws extended. She briefly had the time to realize that she was dead before the wolf hit her and she went down. Claws raked across her shoulder, leaving bloody marks. She felt wolf breath on her face and knew it intended to rip into her. Terror and panic chased through her, but they were overwhelmed by sheer anger.

"No!" she screamed at the creature, something within her refusing to give in to fear and death. Somehow, somewhere, inside of her there was power, power that she could feel growing. In what seemed to be the space of time between one shaky heartbeat and the next, her fingers closed about the amulet she still carried with her. She clutched at it desperately, wondering why she was still alive, why her face hadn't been torn off. The tickle of power she had felt began to grow, flooding out from within, possessing and filling her.

There was a light from somewhere, starting to fill her senses. She could see the face of the wolf, frozen in mid-snarl, just a few inches from her own. The weight of the wolf on her chest somehow seemed lighter and she pushed at it with the fist that grasped the amulet. The wolf toppled backward, a look of fear and panic in the previously hate-filled eyes. It seemed to be getting less substantial and in seconds had simply faded and vanished.

Somehow Andrea managed to regain her feet. It was as if the world were frozen around her. Even the falling snow hovered stiffly in the still air. The wolves were there in mid-leap, held before they could hit their targets, as if captured by the eerie light that was emanating from the amulet in her tight fist. Not really understanding what she was doing, she walked stiffly through the strangeness, her hand held out before her. As she touched the wolves they seemed to lose their weight and substance and to simply blow away into nothingness. One by one, she somehow made them vanish back to whatever they had emerged from. When the party was alone again, she felt the power start to drain from her, taking all of her remaining strength.

"That was well done indeed, my lady," Ulric said, leaping forward to catch her before she struck the iron-hard earth. "They chose wisely when they gave you the amulet of power."

"I don't know what I did," she admitted, weakly. It felt rather nice to be held firmly in those knightly arms.

"You used the power within you, channeled through the amulet," Ulric explained. "But it has severely depleted your strength. I do not know how much more of this you will be able to do."

"It doesn't matter at the moment," Blodwen said, practically. "What she did saved all of our lives." She eyed the knife in her shaking hand. "I don't think we'd have stood a chance otherwise."

"Indeed," said Dr. Ballard, his eyes shining with pride. "I'm very thankful, my dear – even if I don't quite believe it."

"Not only that," Carter observed. "But it looks like the snow is stopping."

"Can that burst of power really have reversed the Outwand's attack?" Blodwen asked.

"It's not all me," Andrea said with certainty. "Look."

With the dying of the snow, visibility had improved considerably. Andrea almost wished it hadn't.

About forty feet away, Caldera was locked in combat with a wolf of his own. This one, however, was even larger than the hell-hound, standing over a dozen feet tall. It was like a huge mountain of white fur, though that whiteness was marred in numerous places by rivulets of bright blood. The wolf and the hound fought in almost total silence, all of their energies and attention focused on the battle. Each struck, snapped and withdrew, the blows and teeth leaving their red trails.

"The Fenris wolf," Dr. Ballard breathed.

"The what?" Carter asked.

"The Fenris wolf," Andrea's father repeated. "In Norse mythology it is one of the monsters that will be unleashed on the day of Ragnarok – the doom of the gods. It is the power of ice and snow that will overwhelm even the power of the gods. To the northmen, the forces of cold were the ultimate victor in the fight."

"I don't think they're winning this one," Andrea said. "Caldera is a creature of heat, don't forget."

Perhaps it was just her wishful thinking, but she felt that her hound was winning the struggle. Caldera was certainly wounded and bore marks that would scar – if he survived the fight. But the Fenris wolf seemed to be getting the worst of it. Perhaps the burst of power she had somehow released had affected it as well as the other wolves, the ones that had clearly been a part of the ice-wolf's pack. Snarling, fighting savagely, the wolf was clearly losing ground. Caldera was forcing it to retreat from the party of humans he was protecting. Andrea clutched at the amulet again. Perhaps if she could summon another burst of power, she could help the hound to win? She started to reach within herself and was startled by a gentle hand on her shoulder.

"No, my lady," Ulric said, firmly. "Each use of power drains you and you must recover before you try again. I know that you wish to help your protector, but you can help no one by over-reaching and killing yourself. I do not think you know how weak you are."

Now that the knight mentioned it, Andrea realized that she was indeed very weak. It was taking most of her strength to simply stand. He might be correct in thinking that another surge of magic might kill her. The energy for magic had to come from *somewhere*, she realized, and that was clearly from her own energy reserves. But Caldera might need her help...

"He's doing well enough," Blodwen said, gently. "And I don't think he'd want you to risk your life further. See."

Her companions were right: Caldera was now clearly winning the battle. The snow seemed to be fading away as a result of the burst of energy she had released, and the great wolf clearly must derive his strength from the ice and cold. Now it was fading, so too was the wolf. Caldera pressed hard, lunging and striking over and again. The Fenris wolf fell back, pace by bloody pace, looking worse for each step. Caldera made a final lunge and tore at the great wolf's throat. Blood flowed like a fountain, and the white beast fell.

Caldera threw back his head and howled in triumph. Then he raised a leg and urinated on his slain foe. Andrea had to stifle a giggle.

The last of the drifting snow faded away, and the wolf slipped into nothingness with it. Caldera walked proudly back to join them and Andrea threw her arms about his neck. "You're the best dog in *any* world," she told him, proudly. "You saved us all." Caldera panted, but seemed proud. Then he winced, and Andrea realized that she was probably squeezing his wounds and promptly let get. He moved off and started licking at his matted fur.

"I've got some medical supplies," Dr. Ballard said. "Carter's mother insisted on packing them, just in case. I can see to his wounds." The hell-hound growled and glared at him, and then went back to licking at himself. "Or I could just
leave him to it," Dr. Ballard decided. "He seems to know what he's doing."

"That attack is over," Ulric said grimly. "But I doubt it will be the end of the Outwand's attempts to stop us. We draw closer now, and it knows we are coming. The next threat may not be dealt with quite as easily."

"*Easily*?" Carter echoed. "Then I don't want to be around when it tries a *difficult* attack."

"It may not have time," Blodwen said, pointing. "I can see the Tor again – we are almost there."

But what would be waiting for them?

Chapter Thirteen

In contrast with most of the towns they'd passed through, Glastonbury was crowded. There seemed to be people everywhere, milling around, talking, and even laughing. Andrea was puzzled by this, and even more so when they actually had to get off their bikes and walk. None of the gathered people seemed to be aware of the attack the travelers had suffered through, barely a mile from this spot. Had these festive crowds noticed nothing? Or was the Outwand blinding their eyes?

At least people made way for Ulric's horse, but nobody seemed at all surprised to see a knight on horseback. It soon became clear why, because a lot of the people as they reached High Street were dressed even more bizarrely.

There were men in long, flowing gowns with stars and moons stitched on them. There were women in gypsy garb and veils. There were even a couple of belly dancers, several "Arabs" in robes, and people dressed in all sorts of ancient clothing, from Roman togas to Medieval dresses. There were even a few in superhero costumes.

"What is this?" Carter asked, staring all around. "A freak convention?"

"It's Glastonbury," Dr. Ballard replied. "It's long since been one of the New Age centers of England. It has always attracted a lot of... shall we say *different-thinking* folks?" He glanced around. "Though never this amount."

"It's the convergence of worlds," Blodwen said. "The apparitions are bringing everyone who knows about this place here."

"It's going to make our task more difficult," Andrea observed. "If they know any of the legends, they're likely to be in all the places we want to be."

"And they're all going to be convinced they need to be there, too," Blodwen agreed. "Lucky I'm with the police, then, isn't it? I can always move them along..."

There was a crowd about the Market Cross, and a man on the

steps there. He was one of those dressed like a wizard, and was preaching to the listening crowd.

"This is the dawn of the Next Age!" he cried, raising his arms. "We have all seen the signs in the sky and on the earth! The present age of science and skepticism, the age of unbelief, is dying. It has been predicted by the sages of old – the Mayans, the Egyptians and the hosts of Atlantis! The Masters from the farther dimensions are speaking to us, and they are telling us that the old way is passing, and the new is being born!" There were choruses of agreement with him.

"They're telling you *everything* is dying, you moron," Carter muttered, quietly, so the enthusiastic supporters of the man wouldn't hear him.

"People are seeking faith," Dr. Ballard said. "And what the Outwand is causing seems to them to be the manifestation of their beliefs."

"They've got rocks in their heads, then," Carter decided.

"They simply think differently to you," Blodwen said."And some of what they believe is valid enough – this is a skeptical and unbelieving age."

"I think they make up for it," Carter replied. "They believe in *everything*."

"I believe we should move on," Andrea said. "Otherwise there soon won't be anything left to believe in. And look on the bright side – one good thing about this lack of electrically-powered equipment is that they can't play CDs. Otherwise I expect we'd have *Aquarius* blasting from everywhere."

They pressed on. The crowds were getting so thick that they reluctantly decided to abandon their bicycles. They were no longer really needed, after all. If they succeeded in their quest, power should be restored and they could rent a car and drive home. And if they failed, the world would come to an end, and then who'd have a use for a bike? Ulric dismounted, and led his steed by hand. The horse's size and weight tended to clear a path in front of it. What surprised Andrea the most was that nobody seemed to think there was anything odd

about Caldera, even though the hound was huge, fearsome and had clearly been in a fight. People would look at him and stare, but then look away again as if they were perfectly used to seeing hell-hounds wandering through the streets.

Well, given what was happening, maybe they were.

There were aging hippies – beads in their hair and floral prints in profusion – everywhere. Many were singing and dancing. Several dozen people seemed to have set up camp in the roads now that there was no traffic flowing. They all seemed happy and caught up in what they thought was the fulfillment of their dreams – the end of the age of skepticism and the dawn of the new era of peace and spirituality.

They had absolutely no idea, Andrea realized.

"I suspect they're smoking something," Blodwen said with a sigh, the police woman in her coming to the fore. "And it's not breakfast kippers."

"We'll worry about that later," Dr. Ballard told her. "We do have more important concerns than making arrests for smoking pot." She nodded, and they pressed on.

The abbey entrance lay off Magdalene Street, through an ancient gateway. Normally there would be someone there taking money for entrance, but today the gates were wide open and the ticket booth abandoned. There were so many people around the attendants had probably given up trying to collect fees. Or attempting to keep any sort of order.

"This is going to be a problem," Blodwen said. "I mean, if we just start hacking at the Christmas Thorn, we might start a wave of vandalism."

"Trust you to think like a cop," Carter grumbled. "If we don't succeed, what difference will it make? And if we do, I think tearing one tree to bits would be a small price to pay for saving the world." That didn't sit too well with Blodwen, but she put up no further argument.

Dr. Ballard, naturally, had memorized the layout of the place. The main part of the abbey was in ruins, with jagged teeth of masonry all that was visible. "Built in the 12th Century," he told them. "And then dissolved by Henry VIII in the 16th Century. A lot of the stones were taken off to build
stuff elsewhere, and most of what was left just rotted."

It seemed a terrible shame. Even with people all over, the place had a sort of wistful beauty. It must have been magnificent when it was first finished. Now it was a ruin, but at least it was one with character. Andrea felt sorry for the poor place.

Her father led them to St. Patrick's Chapel, the only intact building in the grounds. Thankfully, there were fewer people here. "How come?" Carter wanted to know.

"They're all over by the old Choir area," Dr. Ballard explained. "Near to the burial site of King Arthur." He glanced at Ulric, and corrected himself: "Near where King Arthur is *supposed* to be buried. They must feel that's the most sacred spot."

One of the people close by heard this. "No, man," she said, shaking her love-beaded head. "They're there because that's where the monks are."

"Monks?"

"Yeah, real live – uh, well *dead* monks, all chanting. It's a scene of real power, you know. Tripping!"

"More shades of the dead," Ulric said. "They have returned to their home, to carry on what they know."

The woman gave him an admiring look. "Nice costume, man! Where did you buy those threads?"

Ulric looked at her in puzzlement. "They were hand-woven for me, my lady, in Annwyn."

"You'll have to give me the name of the shop, then. Really nice workmanship..."

Blodwen pushed between them. "Sorry, we're kind of busy. No time for fashion chats. We'll catch you later." She looked at the party. "Come *on*. None of this is important. We have to get to the thorn."

It was just ahead of them, a rather straggling, unaesthetic-looking tree. It stood some twenty feet tall, and cast its shade across the chapel wall. Dr. Ballard smiled. "This is certainly not a species native to England. The theories say this is either some sort of a Syrian species, or else a sport bred from an English hawthorn. It doesn't look like either to me."

"It doesn't look like much to me," Carter said.

"It is Caliburn," Ulric said firmly, striding forward and placing his

John Peel

hand against the trunk. "Can you not feel its power?"

Andrea moved to join him, and touched her palm to the trunk. She gasped. A slight shiver passed through her, as if electricity were flowing here. There was a vague, comforting whisper of a voice she couldn't quite hear, and a feeling of well-being. "I can feel it, too," she breathed.

"The magic within it calls to you, my lady," Ulric informed her. "Most would not be able to discern its power, but you are truly gifted." Andrea blushed at his sincere compliment.

Blodwen, then Carter, and finally her father all touched the trunk. Expressions of awe and delight crossed their faces. They could all sense the power and strength here. Either they were all psychic, too, or the magic was growing stronger. Thank goodness that applied to good magic as well as the evil!

"This is our defense," Ulric said, drawing his sword. "We must fashion ourselves wands from it. They cannot contain the full power of Caliburn, but they will provide us with some measure of aid." The others stepped back as he hacked off a branch.

"Here!" said an aggrieved voice. "What do you think you're doing, then? Bloody vandals!" A uniformed man was hurrying toward them. "It's always the same, be nice to people and they take advantage of you! Stop that this instant!"

Andrea groaned. "One of the attendants," she realized. "I knew this would mean trouble."

Ulric ignored the man, and was using his sword to hack off the twigs to make the branch into a walking stick. The official came to a halt, glaring at the knight. "I said stop that!"

Ulric barely looked at him. "This is needed to save the worlds. Please do not attempt to interfere."

"Oh, threats now, is it?" the man demanded. He was about fifty, thin and balding, but he tried to make himself look more imposing by breathing in and pushing out his chest. "I shall have the police on you!"

"I am the police," Blodwen said, moving forward. She flashed her badge at the man. "And this is official business."

The attendant seemed perplexed. "Official vandalism, that's what

127

it is! Stop him immediately!" He spluttered as Ulric handed the first wand to Andrea and calmly cut a second. "Hey, stop it!"

"Please don't interfere, sir," Blodwen said in her crispest, most police-like voice. "As I said, this is official business, and we do know what we are doing. We require five sticks, and then we shall leave the tree alone, I assure you."

"Sticks? I'll give you sticks!" The man looked wildly around. "You're nothing but bloody hooligans, whatever you say, and I'm going to see that you get what you deserve." He hurried off, spluttering and fuming.

"I'd suggest moving a little faster," Blodwen said drily. "Here, you hack off the staves, and I'll trim them." Andrea noted with surprise that Blodwen now had Ulric's knife. How had she gotten that? Oh, right – she'd been wielding it when they fought the wolves. Obviously she simply hadn't given it back. Ulric nodded, tossed Blodwen the branch he'd been working on, and started on a third.

In moments, they each had a four to five foot long stick, rough and a bit hard on the grip, but Andrea could still feel the power flowing through hers. It was like a warmth in her soul, giving her strength and courage. "Will this be power enough against the Outwand?" she asked.

"It will have to be," replied Ulric simply. "It is all that we have. Now, we must find where the Outwand is."

As he spoke, Andrea could feel the staff she held give a slight but perceptible tug toward the south-east. She blinked, and saw that everyone else seemed to be as surprised. "Uh, I think Caliburn is trying to tell us something..."

Dr. Ballard nodded. "Undoubtedly the Tor," he said. "It's exactly where I was going to suggest looking for Mark, anyway. It's a very mystical site, and the logical first place to check out."

"Then let's not hang around here talking," Blodwen decided. "Besides, I think it might be best to be gone when that attendant returns with help. I'm sure I could probably
talk us out of trouble, but I'm equally sure it would be very
time consuming. You know how the official mind is..."

They hastily exited the abbey again, heading south down

Magdalene Road. The people were still milling about, but the crowds thinned as they left the center of town. Andrea could feel the wand she held still pulling her gently. Perhaps this didn't have the full power of Caliburn, but it certainly held power of some kind. They turned into Bere Lane, and she was puffing slightly from the pace they were all keeping up. Blodwen looked a little pale, as her back couldn't possibly have healed yet from the earlier attack and Dr. Ballard was definitely showing the strain from all of this unaccustomed exercise. But Ulric and Carter seemed to be in fine shape. Andrea found herself envying them both. She was still a little tired from her use of magic in the fight. Caldera seemed to be unbothered by his own wounds, though.

At the end of the lane they turned toward the Tor finally, which was quite clearly visible beyond the fields. There were some houses along the street and more people once again. A lot more people, most of them in mystical garb. Some of them seemed to be rather insubstantial. Andrea realized that the fact that they were obviously ghosts didn't seem to be bothering her too much. You could get used to pretty much anything, it seemed – and seeing specters wandering about hardly seemed worth getting upset about right at this minute.

"I was afraid of this," her father said, staring at the crowds. "I'm not the only one who knows the legendary power of the Tor. This could get to be a problem, the closer we get. The New Agers are likely to be jealous of their mystical site."

"We shall deal with it." Ulric didn't seem to have any doubts. Andrea couldn't say the same.

They reached a small New Age gift shop, and the grounds of something called the Chalice Well. More silliness, or something real?

Dr. Ballard gestured. "I feel that we should stop here first," he said.

Andrea could sense the pull of the staff she held leading her the same way. "I get that," she agreed, and so did the rest of the party. With a shrug, she turned into the gate, and followed the flow of people up the slight hill. "What's so special about this place?" she asked her father.

"It's a natural spring that was converted into a well in about the 12th century," he explained. "It's never been known to run dry, and the water contains iron. Legends say it was formed when Joseph of Arimathea laid the Grail here. It's even reputed to have caused miraculous cures."

They passed through the gardens, and reached the well itself. It was stone-lined and slightly sunk into the ground. There was a woman there with a scoop, offering drinks to the gathered people. Ulric raised his staff slightly, and somehow the crowd parted to allow them through.

"We should be grateful for a drink, my lady," Ulric said.

"For you, handsome?" The woman grinned. "Any time." She offered him the scoop, and he drank. Then Blodwen followed, and Andrea. The water tasted funny – due to the iron, of course – but cool, and very refreshing. Carter and then finally her father followed. The woman looked at them and frowned. "Are you here because of the manifestations?" She stared at Caldera. "Or have you brought your own?"

"In a sense," Blodwen agreed cheerfully. "We're in a bit of a hurry, though. Thanks for the refreshment." She turned away. "Time for the Tor," she said with conviction. Andrea could feel the staff she held telling her the same thing. This stopover seemed odd, given the urgency of their quest, but she knew there had to have been some significance to it. Perhaps there really was some sort of power in the well and they were in need of it.

Back on the road, they moved on toward the Tor. The crowds were thicker again, but strangely subdued. Andrea would have expected the unrestrained good humor of the folks in town, or perhaps even panic if something evil had manifested itself. Instead, people seemed to be simply standing about, speaking in lowered tones. Her wand tingled, as if anticipating something ahead.

They reached the field that surrounded the Tor, and saw that the people were all standing back from the approach. Thanks to the wands of Caliburn, the five of them were able somehow to part the bystanders without causing any friction. People simply moved aside, as if of their own free will, to allow them to pass. Once they reached the front of the crowd, Andrea could see what was holding them back and causing them to be so quiet.

There was a ring of armed men, all facing outward, about the base of the hill. They were dressed simply, but some had pieces of metallic armor on. Their weapons looked to be short swords of bronze.

The closest of the men glared at Andrea, and spoke in guttural tones. Surprisingly, Andrea found she could understand him perfectly even though there was no way his words were English. "Stay where you are. No one may approach the holy site at this time. If you come closer, you will die."

Chapter Fourteen

Andrea wasn't sure what they should do now, but Carter stepped forward. "They're obviously just more of the ghosts from the past," he said. "They can't hurt us."

"You're wrong there, mate," said one of the crowd, a youngish man in druid's robes. "They're real, right enough, and they mean what they say."

Andrea pointed at the closest warrior. "If he were a ghost, you'd be able to see something through him," she told Carter. "And you can see his footprints in the grass. He's real enough." And there were a lot of them, too. Even if Ulric could take out some of them, there were too many to consider seriously fighting. Besides which, Andrea had no desire to see a massacre – either of her family and friends or of these soldiers from another age. She looked at Caldera, hoping that the dog would be inclined to fight on their behalf, but he didn't seem to be interested. He was guarding her back as he always seemed to be doing, but he wasn't looking at these warriors as if they were a threat. Did he know something that the rest of them didn't? Or did he just not feel like fighting at this moment? His instincts seemed to be sound, and she knew his bravery was beyond questioning. So why was he acting so unconcerned?

"Well, we can't just stand here," Carter grumbled.

"No, we can't," agreed Blodwen. Clutching her staff firmly, she raised it to eye-level and stepped toward the warrior. "We have been called here," she said firmly. "You have no right to block our passage. Stand aside, and allow us through, onto this mystical hill."

For a second, the warrior looked as if he was going to fight. Then he blinked, and, astonishingly, he did indeed step aside. His eyes were lowered slightly. "That is your right," he agreed, in a subdued tone. "You may pass."

Andrea let her breath out again. She'd been terrified that Blodwen was going to be struck down. She'd grown awfully fond of the police woman over the past few days. She was courageous, and filled with

resolve, and the thought of
seeing her killed was nauseating.

"Come along, then," Blodwen said, as she stepped through the circle of soldiers. None of the other men made any move to stop her either. Ulric, Dr. Ballard, Andrea and finally Carter moved forward also. The druid made to follow them, but the soldier moved back and held up his sword.

"Only the chosen may enter here," he snarled.

"But I'm a *druid*!" the young man protested. "This is one of my sacred sites. I have a right to be here."

"I know nothing of that," the warrior growled. "I know that if you try to pass, then your blood will soak this earth."

"It's not fair!" the young man wailed. "You let them through!" He sounded more like a child than a druid.

"It's a private party," Carter said as they walked on in a tense silence. They all were obviously thinking what Andrea was – that perhaps the soldiers might change their minds about letting them through. They were all heavily armed and not the friendliest of folks.

"Whose side do you think they're on?" Andrea asked Ulric softly about the soldiers.

"Perhaps neither," he said. "The sacred place might have its own guardians, to keep back the uninvited. That is well for us, as I would not wish to have to fight the Outwand with foolish innocents to worry about. They are of an early age than even mine – perhaps even the people who first discovered these sacred sites. They are close to the Earth and its power, and they must have been its guardians at one time. Now the power has reawakened, then so have they. They are attuned to the Tor, and can clearly sense what is allowed here. They recognize our right to enter."

"So they won't interfere with what we do?" she asked anxiously.

"If they are guardians of this Tor, then they might strike against us if they think we are harming it," Ulric said. "Otherwise we should be safe enough – at least from them. They cannot be working for the Outwand, otherwise they would never have allowed us to pass. I am sure that Mara knows Caliburn approaches."

"Great," Carter complained. "Which means it's most likely laying a trap for us."

"That would make sense, yes," Ulric agreed. He didn't seem too concerned about the thought.

"And we just walk into it?" Carter asked. He quite clearly *did* seem concerned.

"We cannot know what the trap is until we spring it," the knight pointed out. "We must be ready for anything, and constantly alert."

"I'd feel happier with something a little more positive than wishful thinking," Carter grumbled.

"We have something," Blodwen said. "Caliburn."

"Which, sad to say, we know is weaker than the Outwand," Dr. Ballard was compelled to add.

"We have no other choice but to press on," Ulric said.

"I know," Andrea's father sighed. "But I can't help wishing for better odds."

The way up the Tor was quite steep, even if the path was worn from centuries of travelers and worshipers. Dr. Ballard couldn't resist being educational, even though he was short of breath. "The Tor is over 500 feet above sea level," he explained. "It's theorized that Arthur and other Britons used it as a watchtower, so to speak, lighting bonfires here for warning." He gestured to the south. "South Cadbury is over there, another tall hill. That's where Camelot was, and Arthur would have been able to see any warning fire set here, to know the enemy was approaching."

"That is what I have been told," Ulric agreed. "There were many tribes who raided the Britons in Arthur's day, and the warning fires were too often lit." He sighed. "Too many good men were lost in such fighting."

"There are other interesting points about the Tor," Dr. Ballard continued. "Though it is a natural hill, it has been shaped by men." He gestured. If you look at the outline of the hill, you can see that it has been cut into terraces. If you were able to look down on the hill from the air, you'd see that these pathways make up the form of a maze."

"What, without bushes to help you get lost?" asked Carter.

"Not that sort of a maze." Dr. Ballard was in full lecture mode now, even as he scrambled to climb. "This is not intended as amusement for children. It is a pathway that the mystics would take, a sacred way of approaching their central mystery. You walk the pathway to draw spiritually closer to your gods. There are even some still around in churches. People are encouraged to walk them and pray. It's a method of focusing the mind on the Holy, a way to help you to cross from this world into the other."

"Maybe we should be approaching the Tor in that way, then?" Blodwen suggested anxiously. "We should do this the right way."

"Not this time," Dr. Ballard said. "To travel the pathway takes more than three hours, I believe, and I do not think we can waste so much time. On the other hand, it might have helped to increase our power. But, anyway, the worlds are so close together now there is little need to go through rituals to approach them. The barriers are already down."

"I suppose you're right," Blodwen agreed. "And also, I want to get this bloody climb over with as soon as possible."

They stopped talking and continued up the steep pathway. There were plenty of rocks to give them grip, and there hadn't been any recent rains to turn the ground to mud. Eventually, though, they came to the summit, and gratefully stepped onto the more level ground. Ahead of them was the shell of the church tower, and beyond that a magnificent view of the surrounding countryside. Standing together, they caught their breaths and looked about.

There was a shimmering over everything they could see, from the houses to the fields and woods. The roads were all virtually clear of traffic, but they seemed somewhat hazy. Andrea felt a sort of scratching at the back of her mind, as if something other than what she was able to see was attempting to intrude. The feeling of barely-leashed power was much stronger here than anywhere they had so far been.

"Heat haze?" asked Carter, puzzled. "The day doesn't seem hot enough for that."

"It isn't," Ulric replied. "We are looking at the breakdown between the dimensions. The worlds are drawing closer together, and portions of Annwyn and the other planes are starting to emerge. Soon the overlap will begin and then everything will be destroyed. We cannot have more than a handful of hours left to us now."

"I'm afraid he's probably right," Dr. Ballard agreed. "Reality as we know it is on a countdown to extinction. We must move swiftly."

"Uh – move to *where*?" Carter asked. "I mean, look around, guys. There's us, and there's that broken-down tower. And that's it. There's no Mark here, and no Outwand. We've been led on a wild goose chase, folks. This is a dead end."

Andrea stared around, and saw that he was quite correct. There was only the five of them here, in the shadow of the old tower.

And nothing and no one else...

John Peel

Chapter Fifteen

Despair clutched at Andrea; after all they had been through, to be so fooled... There was nothing here; somehow, the Outwand had duped them... She had never felt so depressed in her life. She wanted to cry, to howl in frustration.

But then she could feel the gentle flow of strength from the rod she carried. As she concentrated on this, her courage and convictions returned, slowly fanned back to life again. There was a warmth inside her, too, as if she was drawing strength from the drink of well water she had taken earlier.

"No!" she said, decisively. "We haven't been misled. The Outwand is here, all right – we simply can't see it."

"The Lady Andrea is correct," Ulric agreed, with just as much conviction. "Do not forget, the worlds are converging. I believe that the Outlaw Wand has simply moved on from this spot to one of the other worlds."

"Other worlds?" Blodwen blinked. "You mean it's made some sort of a dimensional jump?"

"That's logical," Andrea's father agreed. "The Outwand wants to get at the World Tree, after all, and it can't do that from the Earth. It *must* have moved on, and from this spot somehow."

"That's all well and good," Carter complained. "But *we* can't cross between worlds, can we?"

"Yes, we can," Andrea said. The more she thought about it, the more certain she was that she was right. She took the amulet from around her neck. "Ulric used this medallion to cross from Annwyn to Earth. We should be able to use it to cross from here to wherever the Outwand has gone."

Ulric looked uncertain. "The small store of energy you had was used up when you fought those wolves," he said. "It may be dangerous to your health to use up any more of your energy."

"Then we recharge it," Andrea said. "This is, after all, supposed to be a very mystic place." She held up her staff. "And we have Caliburn, don't we?"

Blodwen gave a delighted laugh. "You know, I think she has something there. And with the dimensions already overlapping because of Mara, then I think it must be a lot simpler now to slip between the worlds than when Ulric did it earlier."

"You're talking *magic*," Carter objected. "And none of us knows how to do that stuff. We're not Harry Potter, you know. We're not even Ron."

"It doesn't matter," Andrea said. "*Caliburn* knows. And I think what I did with the wolves early shows that I do have some sort of control over at least a little magic." The more she focused on this thought, the clearer her course of action was. "All right, everybody gather around me, with your staffs pointed at me. And *think* very hard about opening the way that the Outwand has gone." She stood on the hill, clutching the chain of the medallion, allowing it to swing free in her left hand. In her right, she held her own rod.

Caldera bristled beside her, growling low in his throat. Something seemed to have finally affected him about this place.

"We've got company," Carter said abruptly. "And they don't look friendly."

Andrea followed his pointing finger, and stiffened in shock. On the Tor, she could now see several dozen white-robed forms moving. They hadn't been there when she had looked about a moment before, but now they marched with grim purpose. The leading two and final two figures carried torches that seemed to be blazing brightly even in the daylight. Several others carried a man who was tightly bound.

"They're treading the maze path," Dr. Ballard said softly. "You can see how it winds beneath their feet. They must be druids or pre-druids of some sort."

"They have a captive," Blodwen said.

Dr. Ballard shook his head. "A victim." He gestured toward the tower. Beside it now stood a large, vaguely man-sized cage made from thin wood, and set upon the making of a large fire. "The wicker man. They would take a victim, bind him into that cage and then set it afire, burning him alive, as a sacrifice to their gods."

"We've got to save him!" Blodwen exclaimed.

"It's too late for that, my lady," Ulric said gently. "They are but shades of what once happened. That man was killed thousands of years back, and none of us can now save him. But if these men have been conjured up by the Outwand, then they could probably add us to their victims once they reach us."

Blodwen bit at her lower lip, obviously frustrated that she could do nothing to aid the innocent. "How long before they get here?" she asked Dr. Ballard.

He studied their movement. "About fifteen minutes, I'd say."

"They've already noticed us," Carter warned them. One of the druids had looked up in alarm, and was gesturing toward the summit of the Tor now. He was a younger man, his face twisted with rage. "I'm assuming he's thinking something like *death to the defilers...*"

That was undoubtedly true. As they watched, the youth turned to rush up at them, a sickle-shaped blade in his hand. One of the other druids attempted to restrain him, but the man was too incensed. Breaking from the path, he started to dash toward the top of the hill. He left footprints as he moved, so he was clearly not just a ghost.

Andrea almost laughed. To be thinking something like *he's not just a ghost* showed how weird things had become.

"Trouble," Carter warned.

Abruptly, the young druid stopped. He half-turned, and then screamed.

Something blotted out the light, and a dark, amorphous shape settled across the druid. He screamed again, collapsing to the earth and writhing. There was the sound of tearing, and then the shadow was gone.

The broken body of the druid, steaming slightly, lay on the ground. Blood streamed from a hundred wounds that had been torn into his flesh by unseen talons.

"That's why the druids had to walk the sacred maze," Dr. Ballard breathed. "Their angry god, Woden, lay in wait if they broke the ritual."

"Maybe it's a good thing, then, that we didn't try to walk the maze," Blodwen said quietly. "That could have happened to us..."

"I think we can assume there won't be any further interruptions till they reach the brow of the hill," Andrea's father said, his voice catching slightly. "That being the case, I *really* think we should get on with this attempt to open the gateway to follow the Outwand."

They needed no further encouragement. The other four gathered about Andrea, and she held the amulet up. "Cardinal points," she suggested.

"Good thinking," her father approved. He took north; Ulric moved south; Carter took east and Blodwen west. They all raised their wands, pointing them toward Andrea. She held her own wand vertically, and the medallion high.

Concentrate... she ordered herself. They needed to find where the Outwand had fled... It had to have been from here, and the pathway should still be there, only hidden from mortal sight. But they had the aid of Caliburn, and the power of good on their side. The gateway must appear. It *must!*

There was a stirring of the air about them, and a strong breeze caught Andrea's hair. She felt her excitement rising as the wind kicked up.

"I hope this is our magic, and not this Woden getting blood-thirsty again," Carter muttered.

"This is the good," Andrea replied, with absolute conviction. "Can't you feel the power passing through you?" She could feel the growth of *something*, a strength and purpose far beyond her own small abilities. Caliburn was drawing its power, seizing the fabric of reality and twisting it to their purposes. The everyday world was breaking down, and their power was calling upon it to obey their needs.

There was a loud crash, and the ground shook. Andrea gazed about her, helpless to act. The earth shuddered again, and then split, the crack starting just outside their circle and leading toward the tower. The ground steamed, and the power slowly died away.

"Wow, we caused an earthquake, folks," Carter announced. He was shaking slightly. "I don't see how that helps us in any way."

"Because you will not see," Ulric chided him gently. "That was no simple shaking of the earth." he gestured with his staff. "That is the

140

pathway to Annwyn, my home."

"Annwyn?" Carter's voice got a little squeaky. "Annwyn as in *land of the dead*?"

"That is one aspect of it," Ulric agreed, unconcerned. "There is more to it, however. The Outwand has crossed to Annwyn because that is the way to Yggdrasil. It has passed that way, and we must follow."

"We must?" Carter asked, weakly. "Aren't there any other options?"

"Stay behind if you'd rather," Andrea said. She could feel in her heart that Ulric was correct; *this* was where their path led. She had no option but to walk it if she wanted to find her brother again. And, of course, save the worlds from self-destructing.

"No, no, I didn't say that." Carter moved closer to her. "It just seems a little... *foolish*, shall we say?"

"It probably is," agreed Blodwen. "But what other choice do we have?"

"None," agreed Andrea's father. "And, personally, I find the chance of visiting the land of the dead to be rather exciting. Even if there is a good chance we'll not come back again." He blinked as Blodwen glared at him. "Uh, I mean, of course, I'm sure we'll be fine."

Carter gulped. "Of reference a lack to the chance of coming back," he recited. "*The Pirates Of Penzance*. Very nervous policemen." He glanced at Blodwen. "Nothing personal."

"No offense," she replied. "I'd be lying if I said I wasn't in a highly nervous state." She grinned, somewhat strained. "A policeman's lot is not a happy one..."

"This isn't going to get easier," Andrea said. Holding the amulet high, she stepped toward the fissure in the ground. She could see that it sloped downward, but nothing more than that. It was too dark within. "Anyone remember to bring a flashlight?"

Blodwen chuckled, and drew one out of her knapsack. Of course she had one – she seemed to be prepared for almost any eventuality. She clicked it on, and directed the beam into the gaping hole. Even with that help, they could see no more than about ten feet.

"I shall go first," Ulric decided, drawing his sword.

"No," Andrea said, reluctantly. "I have the amulet; it has to be me. I think you'd better guard the rear. We've wasted so much time those druids are almost here." The knight nodded, and moved to allow her to pass.

Caldera growled again, and nuzzled at Andrea. She looked into his face. He moved off a few feet, his back to them, facing outward. "He's staying to guard our backs," Andrea realized. "I don't think any of those druids will get past him."

"I think he's just scared to go down into the hole," Carter said. "And very sensible of him, too." That was just Carter talking, Andrea knew – the dog was not afraid of anything. Unlike her...

She reached out and threw her arms about Caldera's neck. "You're a good dog," she reassured him, grateful that he was watching out for them. He looked at her, clearly unused to any such sentiment. She doubted that Herne had ever bothered to spend quality time with his animals. Then he abruptly licked her. It was like being drenched in the shower, but she knew it was well meant – if somewhat icky. She let him go again and he moved back to stand guard. She knew that she was correct – nothing would get past him to attack them from the rear. She realized she was going to miss him being with them, but summoned up her courage.

Andrea stepped into the hole, finding the steaming earth firm beneath her feet. She'd been half-afraid it would just collapse and she'd plunge down to her death. Only her confidence in the power and goodness of Caliburn had given her the strength to take that step. Blodwen fell in behind her, then Carter, then Dr. Ballard. Ulric brought up the rear, scanning for anyone following them, in case someone did somehow get past Caldera.

There was the scent of fresh earth all about them and Andrea shuddered as she walked on. It felt as if she was being buried, heading down into the grave... She shuddered as this ominous thought settled in her mind. Perhaps she *was* heading for her own grave. The Outwand was ahead somewhere, its malevolence spreading. It wanted her and the rest of them dead, and knew they were on its trail. Perhaps it had set a trap, and death was in wait for them ahead...

Andrea shook off those terrible thoughts. It was the Outwand, simply trying to scare her into giving in. She refused to allow that to happen. *It's scared we can beat it,* she told herself, drawing comfort from that thought. That was why it was trying to discourage them.

"Don't listen to those thoughts," she whispered to herself.

"How did you know I was getting them?" Blodwen asked, her own voice as quiet.

"We all are," Andrea said.

"It is an attack," Ulric said simply. "The Outwand is attempting to frighten us, as if we were children to be frightened of the dark."

"I *am* a child," Carter complained. "And, trust me, it's not stupid to be afraid of *this* dark."

There was a sudden scream of laughter, echoing about them. It rubbed Andrea's nerves badly, and she shivered. There was no telling where the sound had originated. It might be the druids behind them, or something ahead in the darkness of the earth.

Then there was another crash, and the ground shook once more. Carter howled wordlessly, and pointed up.

The slash of daylight sky above them was growing smaller and smaller. The crevasse in the earth was filling in. Andrea felt sheer terror wash over here as the ground filled in. In seconds, they were totally entombed within the dank earth.

Chapter Sixteen

Andrea had to fight back the wave of panic that threatened to engulf her. They were completely trapped within the earth, buried alive God knew where. The stench of the grave was about them, and she started gasping for breath. She could see in the small sphere of light cast by Blodwen's flashlight that the faces of her companions reflected her own horror.

"It's the Outwand," Carter gasped. "It's making us despair again! Don't let it! God, I'm terrified enough as it is, without its help. But I'm not going to let it beat me down."

Andrea felt strengthened; Carter was right: the Outwand wanted them to be convinced that they could never win. Instead she gripped her staff more firmly, and tried to draw from its power. "He's right," she gasped. "It's not as bad as it appears. We're *not* buried alive. It just seems like that."

"That's right," Blodwen said, trying to sound convinced. "We still have air to breath, and a pathway to follow. We'll get out of this."

"Yes," Ulric agreed. "My ladies, the two of you are inspirational. We shall press on, and the Outwand will discover that it cannot cause us to despair."

Andrea swallowed, and summoned up all of her remaining courage. She felt infinitely better when Blodwen slipped her hand into Andrea's and squeezed encouragingly. Together they moved on, and the men followed behind. They were silent, however, none of them wanting to speak in the stillness of the earth.

The light only penetrated about six or eight feet, and there was nothing to see but soil. It was hardly exciting or encouraging, but Andrea refused to allow it to get to her. She just plodded on, holding Blodwen's hand and praying for some change for the better.

She could see vague roots in the earth. They were not on a pre-existing path, but travelling through a gash ripped in the bowels of the planet. The stench of fresh earth filled her nostrils. Thoughts of this being her grave still gnawed at her

mind, despite every attempt to believe that it was not so.

She had no idea how long they walked on the tomb-like path, but suddenly her foot struck something. A rock? "Shine the light down," she asked Blodwen, who did so.

It wasn't a rock; it was a flattened stone, and there were more beyond it. Encouraged by the signs that someone had been here before them, they moved a little faster. Soon the ground was completely paved, and then the walls started showing signs of bricks.

"We're getting somewhere," Dr. Ballard said excitedly.

"But where?" asked Carter.

"We'll soon find out." Andrea was vastly relieved now there were walls about them. She'd been terrified that the earth would simply give way as they walked, collapsing and burying them. Now she felt more secure, and a weight lifted from her nerves.

A short while later they came to a door. Andrea tried it, and it opened into a corridor. Set into the walls at intervals were burning torches, casting a flickering, friendly glow over the place.

"I know this place," Ulric said in wonder. "We are in the castle of the Lady of the Lake."

"Wow," Carter muttered. "How can you tell? It just looks like any moldy old passageway to me."

"The sconces," Ulric explained, ignoring the sarcasm. "See, at the base, they carry the sigil of the Lady." He pointed to a small crest, showing a swan on a lake.

"So you know where to go from here?" asked Andrea eagerly. They were getting free of the tomb, back to some sort of land of the living, even if it was no longer exactly on Earth.

"Follow me." Ulric took the lead. Blodwen extinguished her flashlight and slid it back into her pack. They all fell in behind the hurrying knight.

"Why isn't there anyone around?" asked Andrea.

"We are deep in the bowels of her castle, my lady," Ulric explained. "Few people have reason to come down here."

""Then why are there torches lit here?" Carter

demanded.

"Magic," the knight answered. "They light when they are needed. As I said, there are still magicians amongst our brotherhood here, and they can do simple spells."

"He's got an answer for everything," Carter muttered.

"This way," Ulric said, as they came to a branching corridor. The way to the right had steps leading upward. "We shall be among friends here," he promised them. "And the Lady keeps a good table – we shall feast well this day." He seemed eager, and Andrea couldn't blame him – he must be missing his friends and the comfort of being in his own world. But it wasn't right.

Andrea shook her head. "No," she said gently. "My wand is tugging me. It wants us to go the other way."

Ulric looked puzzled. "Mine also," he agreed. "But there is nothing down there that we should see."

"I think Caliburn would disagree," Blodwen said drily. "What *is* down there?"

"The Waiting Place, my lady."

Blodwen raised an eyebrow. "Would you care to explain that cryptic comment?"

The knight shrugged. "It is forbidden for us to go there," he said. "It is where the King lies, healing, ministered by the Lady and her maidens."

"The King?" Andrea gasped. "Arthur himself?"

"The same, Lady Andrea."

There was a surge in her spirit, a joyous wave, a certainty. "That is where we must go," she said firmly. "I feel it quite definitely."

"So do I," Blodwen agreed. "Wonderful. We get to look in on the medieval equivalent of the local emergency room..."

Ulric was struggling with his instructions, shaped into him from his youth. "We are not supposed to go there," he protested. "It is forbidden to all mortals. Yet I, too, feel the urge. I trust Caliburn knows what it does, else we shall be in dire trouble." He plunged on ahead.

"Like we aren't already?" Carter muttered as he followed along.

The walls were all rough-cut stone, and the sconces

146

with torches quite far apart. There were no side doors, and no further turns. Instead, some two hundred feet later, the passageway ended in a massive oaken door.

On the floor before it was a slumped form. Andrea knew the guard was dead before she saw the dried pool of blood beneath the corpse and the knife through the heart.

"The Outwand has indeed been here," Ulric said grimly, pausing to examine the dead man. "This is Anarik – he was a good, faithful man. But why does the Outwand pass this way?"

"Perhaps to slay Arthur?" Dr. Ballard suggested. "According to the legend, he is to return in the house of England's greatest need to fight his next battle. I should think that a collision of all of the worlds might well be that greatest need."

"And the Outwand wanted to prevent that?" Blodwen asked. "It makes horrible sense. Arthur back alive and in charge would be a most potent force for good."

"We must find out," Ulric said. Grasping the huge door handle, he turned it and shoved open the heavy wooden door.

There were torches ablaze inside the room ahead of them, filling it with flickering light. More of that small magic, obviously. Andrea moved forward behind the knight, and stood inside the room, astonished.

It was some two hundred feet long, and half as wide. The ceiling, curved and vaulted, was about forty feet above them. There were no windows and no other doorway. The entire floor area was filled simply with what looked like tombs. Andrea had seen plenty of these in England – the bodies would be placed within, and on the top, carved from stone, would be a knight or a lady in a long gown, usually with their feet on a small dog. This room had to contain at least a hundred of these.

Then she realized that she was wrong: these were not tombs. The knights and ladies atop them were not carved statues – they breathing, although very slowly. They were *beds* of stone, with sleeping figures atop them. Dozens of unconscious people...

"Dear Lord," Dr. Ballard murmured. "These are the Knights of the Round Table?"

"Those that survived the battle with Modred," Ulric agreed. "My father and mother are here. Many wives are here also. They chose to sleep with Arthur, to be ready to waken and serve him when he has need of them. We children elected to remain awake, to train and be prepared for when our day would arise."

"As a researcher, I *have* to see Arthur," Dr. Ballard said eagerly. "Where is he, Ulric?"

"Over here." He may never have been in this room before, but he clearly understood the layout of the place.

Their footsteps echoed throughout the otherwise-silent chamber. The chamber felt more like a crypt than a hospital, and Andrea found herself moving as quietly as possible, and barely breathing. They moved through the sleeping knights and their ladies to the center of the room. Here were two stone tables larger than the others. On one lay a beautiful woman, dressed in simple but clearly expensive robes.

On the other lay Arthur himself.

Andrea caught her breath as she gazed down at this famous legend, still caught halfway between life and death even after all these centuries. Leather armor lay beside his stone bed, and he wore loose trousers and a tunic. There were bandages across his side, stained slightly with fresh blood where he had been mortally wounded in that last great battle more than a thousand years ago. He looked a little pale, but breathed slowly and easily. His hair and neat beard were both black, with the slightest flecks of grey in them. His face was handsome and barely lined by age. Around his waist was fixed an empty scabbard.

"Now I see why we were led here," Ulric said urgently. He pointed to the scabbard. "Excalibur is gone!"

Dr. Ballard frowned. "I thought your father was supposed to have thrown it into the lake, where the Lady of the Lake reclaimed it?"

"My father did indeed cast the sword as you said, lest it fall into the hands of Modred's men and be used for evil. You see, Excalibur has its own magic. Whenever it is used, it will
cut down whatever foe it faces without fail. We could not allow this to fall into the wrong hands. But when Arthur was brought here, to the Lady's castle, then she restored the sword to the one man pure enough to wield it. It was thought that this would be the safest place to keep it. But now it

is missing."

"The Outwand..." Blodwen said.

"Yes," Ulric agreed. "It wants Excalibur for some purpose of its own. We must recover it; without Excalibur, how can the King return to his rightful glory?"

"But why would the Outwand need Excalibur?" Andrea asked, confused. "Surely it has enough power of its own?"

"Probably," the knight agreed. "But by stealing Excalibur, it may be protecting itself. If this is the threat that Arthur is to rise for, then he will be much less powerful without Excalibur."

"If this is the threat that Arthur's to rise for," Carter said drily, "then I think his alarm clock has been set wrong. There's no sign of any of these sleeping beauties wakening." He eyed Guinevere with interest. Even though she had to be in her late thirties, she was still a regal beauty. "Maybe I should try kissing one and see what happens?"

"You keep your lips to yourself," Andrea snapped. "That's not part of these stories." She was surprised by how angry that silly comment had made her.

"We must move on," Ulric said. "We now know we must recover Excalibur also, and time is growing short."

"Speaking of the shortness of time," Andrea said, worried, "something occurs to me. Back in our world, we had only a few hours until the worlds collided. And you said that time passes far more slowly here in Annwyn. Doesn't that mean we'd have even less time here to stop the Outwand? A day here is like a year in our world, isn't it?"

"Normally, yes," Ulric agreed. "But with the worlds drawing closer, so are their time frames. The time here is now almost equal to the time in your world. If you go back in two days, only two days will have passed there, not two years."

"That's a relief," Dr. Ballard muttered. "I doubt I'd still have a job otherwise. If, of course, our normal world survives all of this and any of us have jobs to go back to."

"But we still don't have the time to waste just standing here and talking," Blodwen pointed out. "Where should we go from here, Ulric?"

He looked at his staff. Andrea could feel the gentle tug from her own. "Back the way we came," he said. "We were led here only so that we might understand what is happening and what is now at stake."

Andrea felt a great relief when they left the room and closed the door. It had been very creepy in there, almost like standing among ghosts. Actually, considering they'd been doing quite a lot of that lately, it was worse than standing among ghosts. It had felt uncanny and terribly intrusive. Ulric knelt briefly beside the dead sentry. "You will be avenged," he promised the man. Then he looked up. "We must go to the castle proper now." He set off down the corridor, back to the turn with the stairs. He hurried up them, and out the door at the top.

They were clearly in an area meant for the living now. There was more light and large windows in the corridor they emerged into. There was the sound of people moving and talking, and that felt wonderful. After what they had just seen, real, living people was just what they needed.

"This way," Ulric said, striding off to the right. They all followed him as he walked swiftly. People passed by, with food, or other items. Some greeted Ulric, others hurried along. After a short walk, they came to large double doors, with two attendants standing ready. "I must see the Lady," Ulric told the men.

The men nodded, and opened the door. Ulric marched inside, and the others trooped in behind him.

This room was what Andrea had always imagined a castle should be like. There were large tapestries on the wall, scenes of hunting and riding, all greens, reds and golds. Large windows shed light across the room, which was some forty feet long and twenty wide. There were seats, most of them empty, lining the walls, and courtiers in livery, all with the swan emblem on their tunics.

There were several men, all clearly knights like Ulric, and a number of very well-dressed ladies. And on a dais at the far end of the room there was a throne, and the Lady was seated upon it, regarding them with surprise and pleasure. She was the most beautiful woman Andrea had ever seen. Her fair hair was long and free, falling about delicate shoulders. Her face was pale and blue-eyed, without any blemishes. Her body showed perfect proportion, and she was quite tall, even seated. She seemed to radiate grace and strength.

"Sir Ulric!" she exclaimed, and her voice was melodious and warm. "I had not expected to see you back so soon."

"I had not expected to be back, Lady," he said, going to one knee and bowing. "Yet I bring grave news. The Outwand has been found and is working its mischief, as we feared. The guard at the Waiting Place lies dead, and Excalibur is stolen."

"Stolen?" The Lady of the Lake rose to her feet with a gasp. She looked about the room. "Sir Pryam, lead a search immediately of the castle! And post a stronger guard at the Waiting Place."

"At once, my Lady!" The chosen knight hurried from the room, and several of his fellows accompanied him.

"I think it's a bit late for that," Blodwen said. "The Outwand has what it came for, and I really don't think it would hang about here to be caught."

The Lady raised a delicate eyebrow. "I do not believe I know your companions, Sir Ulric," she said gently.

"Forgive me, Lady." Ulric gestured as he introduced each. "This is the Lady Blodwen. She is, despite her sex, a warrior in her world. Then this is the Lady Andrea, who has some uncommon skills with magic and wisdom. The Lord Ballard, a teller of tales and a man of knowledge. And the squire, Carter, who serves the Lady Andrea."

"How come *you're* a lady, and I'm just a squire?" Carter grumbled to Andrea.

"Attitude," she shot back, as she curtsied — a skill she never expected she'd ever use. "My Lady," she added, more
loudly.

"You are all welcome here," the Lady of the Lake said warmly.

"I wish we could stay," Andrea said. "But as Blodwen said, the Outwand has gone." She could feel this to be true from her staff. It tugged gently toward the door. "We have to follow it. It has possessed my brother, and I must get him back."

"If he is possessed by it, there is little chance that you will be able to recover him," the Lady said sadly. "You must face the probability that to destroy the Outwand you must also destroy him."

"No!" Andrea and her father both said together. "He's my brother," Andrea went on. "I *must* be able to save him."

"I pray that you are right, but fear that you are wrong." The Lady looked at Ulric. "What will you do now?"

"We must go where we are led." He held up his staff. "These are cut from Caliburn, and they know the way we must go."

"I shall send more knights with you, then," the Lady decided.

"They might be more hindrance than help," Blodwen said, regretfully. "We don't have any more of the good wands to protect them or lead them. Besides, you might need them here. The Outwand is up to something, and it's obviously afraid that Arthur can stop it. Who knows, it might inspire someone to lay siege to this castle or something."

"Very well," the Lady agreed. She sighed. "I wish there was something more I could do to help you, though."

"Pray for us, my Lady," Ulric suggested. "And pray that we might all meet here again when we are successful."

"Optimist," Carter muttered.

"We'd best be going," Blodwen said firmly. "We'd like there to be something here to come back to."

"Yes, my lady," Ulric agreed. He raised his staff. Andrea raised hers, touching its end to his. The others followed suit. Andrea didn't know why, she simply felt that this was the right thing to do. The ladies of the court and the remaining knights fell back.

There was a humming sound coming from the five fragments of Caliburn, and Andrea could feel the power flowing. It seemed to be being drawn here from all parts of the world, flowing through her, channeled into her staff. If this was what it felt like to hold the Outwand, she could understand why Mark had been so grimly determined and so absorbed. It felt exhilarating. She had never felt so alive, so *real*!

Light gathered where the five wands met, and grew in brightness and size. A globe of pure, spinning energy formed, and then sank to the floor. It flashed brightly, and then dissipated.

In the floor of the chamber there was now a large hole, leading downward into the earth.

"Haven't we done this before?" complained Carter.

"That's the way ahead," Andrea informed him. "It's where the Outwand has gone, and where we have to follow."

Blodwen grunted, pulled her flashlight from her knapsack and started down without looking back. One of the knights brought a blazing torch, which he handed to Ulric. Andrea followed Blodwen, and Carter scuttled after her. Her father and then finally Ulric stepped into the pit. They all walked forward, following the pathway downward. It seemed to be no more than a tunnel carved into the ground. It was neither paved nor walled.

They had gone about thirty feet when the light from behind them was cut off. Andrea glanced back, and saw that the opening had sealed itself again. They were isolated once more from the surface world. And their staffs tugged them gently onward.

To where?

Chapter Seventeen

Andrea didn't like going downward into the earth any more this time than she had before. Sticking close to Blodwen, she drew warmth and courage from her wand. She could feel that this was the way that they had to go – but nothing could make her like it.

"Why couldn't the Outwand go somewhere bright and cheery?" Carter grumbled. "The Bahamas, for example?"

"That is not the nature of evil," Ulric said, treating the question seriously. "Foul deeds prefer the darkness. Besides, it wishes to attack the World Tree, and that must perforce have its roots deep within the world."

"Oh, great," Carter sighed. "So now we're on a journey to the center of the Earth."

"Hardly that far," Andrea said, hoping to comfort him. "The Outwand isn't too far ahead of us now. I can somehow sense it."

"It is the magic," Ulric informed her. "As I told the Lady, you have a certain skill with wizardry."

"I thought you were just flattering me to make me sound more important," Andrea said, surprised.

"I have no need to flatter you to make you more important!" the knight protested. "You are the one through whom the magic speaks the loudest. You are the one who guides us with Caliburn."

"Oh." That was something new for her to assimilate. Andrea wondered if he was right or simply being naive. Still, she did seem to be doing some things magical this day, and she could certainly feel *something*, including the knowledge that Mara was only a short distance ahead of them. But *short* as compared to what?

This tunnel seemed to be quite wide and straight, and that clearly bothered Blodwen. "How come this passageway is so convenient?" she asked. "I mean, did the magic create it, or was it here beforehand?"

"What do you mean?" asked Dr. Ballard.

"Well, it's like it was carved out of the ground," the police woman replied. "And if the magic didn't cut it – who did?"

Blodwen had a point, Andrea realized. The tunnel was far too regular to have been formed by any natural activity. It was like something a huge mole might dig... But it would have to be a mole forty feet long to create something like this... The concept of so large a creature would have been ludicrous just days ago. Now – who could be certain that it couldn't exist? The thought of meeting up with it was hardly appealing.

"Can't anyone around here think of something cheerful?" Carter complained. "Or is depression and panic the order of the day?"

"It's the Outwand," Dr. Ballard said. "It must be trying to discourage us from following it once again."

"I'm already discouraged," Carter pointed out. "It should know it doesn't need to work so hard."

"Shush!" Blodwen snapped, holding up a hand and halting. "I thought I heard something ahead."

They stopped, and Andrea held her breath, listening. Blodwen was right; there was some sort of sound from before them, but she couldn't make it out.

"I had better take the lead," Ulric said, moving past them. He handed the torch he carried to Andrea, and held his sword at the ready. "At this juncture it is unlikely that whatever lies before us is friendly."

"Great," Carter sighed. "More depressing thoughts."

There was a sudden rush of noise farther down the tunnel, and then a blur of motion. With a yell, Ulric leaped forward, slashing. Andrea could see only the vaguest of shapes. It looked spindly and spidery, but it must have been at least six feet tall, and was a pallid white color. Something snapped, and growled, and then skittered back, out of the reach of the sword.

"What the hell was that?" Carter gasped.

"I think *hell* might indeed be the appropriate word," Dr. Ballard agreed.

"It looked like the mother of all spiders to me," Blodwen said, her voice shaking slightly.

"Some sort of scavenger," Andrea's father suggested. "White, because it never goes into the sunlight. It must have smelled food. Us."

Ulric was standing wary guard, but the thing didn't seem to be in any hurry to return. "I hope that I have persuaded it that we are not appropriate feasting."

"I hope so, too," Andrea agreed fervently. "Did you get it?"

"I wounded it," he replied, showing her a trail of slimy blood on the edge of his weapon. "It will not attack us again so swiftly."

"I hope it doesn't attack us again, period," Carter said.

"We'd better start moving." Blodwen suited her actions to her words, but she carefully kept behind Ulric. "I'm starting to wish we'd thought to bring a few more weapons with us."

"Yeah, like a flame-thrower or a rocket launcher," Carter agreed. "Do you think those overgrown spiders made these tunnels?"

"Unlikely," Dr. Ballard said. "On Earth, insects inhabit the burrows of many animals. It's probably the same here."

"I'd hate to run into the rabbit that built this place," Carter commented.

"It might not be something as harmless as a rabbit," Dr. Ballard pointed out.

"Great, just what I needed – more depressing thoughts." Carter sank into silent gloom again. This business was clearly really getting to him. He was normally a cheerful person, and full of life. He'd been a lot of fun as a guide and a friend. Since their quest had begun, though, he'd transformed into a brooding, worried soul. Well, Andrea could hardly blame him – this was not an adventure to create laughter and joy. But she missed the old Carter. He showed through from time to time in flashes of humor – but now, even those were dark.

They walked on in their small circle of light, and Andrea listened for any further hints that there might be more monsters in the darkness. She knew that without the support
and encouragement she was drawing from Caliburn she would probably have broken down, crying hysterically, long ago. This was simply too nerve-wracking. Thankfully, anything in the darkness seemed to be staying clear of their small party. Perhaps whatever lurked here thought they were tougher than they really were. Andrea wished it was that they really *were* tough!

"There's a light ahead," Blodwen announced, abruptly. "A sort of a glow, really, I'd say."

Andrea strained to make it out, and saw a vague redness. The tunnel still hadn't branched out, so they had no option but to continue on their way. It finally opened into what appeared to be a central nesting place, but, thankfully, there was no sign of whatever had built the nest. It looked very deserted, in fact.

"No scat," Dr. Ballard observed. "No bedding material. I think whatever built this nest abandoned it a long while ago."

"Why?" asked Blodwen.

Dr. Ballard gestured in the direction the light was coming from. "I'd say that there was an earthquake – or an Annwynquake – a while back, and part of that tunnel collapsed. Maybe the creature doesn't like light. If it lives this far underground, that's quite likely."

The tunnel with the red glow was only one of six that led from the nest, but Andrea could feel from the staff that it was the way they should take. "At least the spider-thing probably took a different tunnel," she pointed out thankfully. "It doesn't care for the light, either."

"Then I'm all for plunging ahead," Carter said with enthusiasm. "I'm not that fond of normal-sized spiders, and it doesn't look as if the word *normal* applies to anything down here. I just hope that there's nothing worse waiting for us ahead." He glared at Ulric. "And don't bother telling us there's bound to be, because of the Outwand. I'll just take it as understood."

"Let's move on," Blodwen decided. She clicked off her flashlight; with the torch and the glow, there was plenty of light to see by. Sliding the flashlight back into her pack, she led the way.

It was a short walk to where the collapse had occurred, and they could all see why the animal had abandoned its burrow. The wall had fallen where it had been perilously close to a natural tunnel, and they could simply step out into the cavernous space. The rocky region ran for a considerable space on either side. They were on a high ledge, and when they looked down...

"Lava," Dr. Ballard said, surprised. "We're in the body of some kind of a volcano."

About two hundred feet down, thick, glowing lava crawled. It was

157

what was causing the glow, and a certain measure of heat. The molten rock below was sluggish, but in motion.

"A *live* volcano," Carter pointed out. "We're *inside* a live volcano. Excuse me, but this is *insane*." He was practically dancing from nervousness.

"It's where we have to be," Andrea informed him. She gestured to the left. "We have to head this way. No matter how scary it may be."

"Wonderful. And if the volcano blows? Don't any of you people watch the late movies? When anyone heads into hidden worlds with a volcano nearby, it's a sure plot hint that the damn thing's going to erupt."

"At least you won't be cold," Andrea snapped. He was really starting to annoy her now. Or was it just that the Outwand was creating friction between them all to slow them down? "Stop complaining, and let's move." She wasn't quite as brave herself as she tried to appear. They were, as Carter had said, inside a potentially disastrous situation here. Even without the threat of the Outwand, being stuck inside a live volcano was wildly horrific. She wanted nothing more than to run the other way, to get out of here. But she couldn't give in to that fear. Too much depended on their success. If it weren't for the comfort she felt from Caliburn she'd have given up long ago. Somehow she couldn't give in the despair and fear while she held her wand.

Blodwen led them off once more. Andrea was sweating slightly, partly from the heat and partly from sheer fear. She'd never been very good with heights, and knowing what would await her at the bottom of any fall didn't help. The ledge, thankfully, was a good ten feet wide, so they didn't need to walk close to the edge and look down at the lava. But there was no ignoring its presence. Knowing it was there made every step seem like it could plunge them down into the volcanic depths, even though the ground seemed perfectly firm. This was definitely not on her list of fun things to do.

Silently, they marched. The pathway was descending slightly as they walked. How long could this go on for? Andrea tried not to worry; Caliburn would hardly lead them down into the lava. Anyway, they couldn't possibly get too close before the heat would be too great. They were still high enough above it so that it was just warm here, but as they got closer, the temperature would start rising.

There were side tunnels, some barely more than cracks in the rock, and some of which had collapsed, probably in the quake that had breached the nest. Andrea looked down at the dirt and gasped.

"Someone's been here before us," she said. In the ground, quite clearly, there were markings of prints.

"Mark, obviously," Dr. Ballard said, excitement in his voice.

"Not unless his shoe size has changed," Carter commented. "Whatever made those prints must be at least a size twenty..."

"And look at the prints," Andrea added. "They're bare feet."

"You mean *people* live down here?" asked Blodwen, incredulously.

"I doubt very strongly they're *people*," Andrea said.

"Oh, great," Carter muttered. "My creepiness factor just went right off the scale. Thanks so much."

"Stop being such a wimp," Andrea said. "We don't have any choice here. We have to go on."

"Yes, but we don't have to like it." Carter sighed, and started forward. "This trip just keeps on getting better and better..."

They moved on again, slowly working their way downward. The red glow cast eerie shadows as they moved, and the miles of rock around and above them seemed to be pressing down upon them. The temperature was rising as they went on, and Andrea's clothing was damp with sweat. More and more, she consoled herself with the thought of a long, cool bath when this was over...

And then the pathway started to get smaller. They were being crowded ever nearer the drop into the river of fire below them. Their safety factor was eroding. Despite her fears, though, Andrea could sense that Caliburn was leading them on. Somehow this was still the right way, despite the increasing evidence to the contrary,

Maybe the wand isn't powerful enough to know the right way, she thought to herself. It was only a small portion of Caliburn, after all, and its magic was that much diminished. Were they being deluded by a false pathway? She looked at Carter, who was even more worried than she was, and then at Blodwen. The police woman was sweating, and her pretty face was very tense. She was obviously having doubts, too. Their eyes linked and Blodwen sighed.

"It's the Outwand," she said. "It's still attacking our minds."

Of course! That was why she was having such troubling thoughts! She should remember that, but clearly Mara was blotting out her memories as well as stoking her fears.

Unless, of course, she was just coming to her senses and realizing how foolish this whole thing was...

Stop it! she ordered herself ferociously. Doubt at this point could be a killer. But still they were getting closer to the lava, and the pathway was getting thinner.

"There's some kind of bridge ahead," Blodwen announced. "Look."

About ten feet ahead of them was a finger of rock that reached from this side of the tunnel to the far side. It was difficult to see whether the pathway on that side was wider than this, but Andrea could feel the urging from her staff to
cross the stone bridge.

Right – cross over on a flimsy bridge, a hundred feet or so above molten lava! One slip of the foot, and she'd fall to a horrible death! There was no way she was going to even try this!

The Outwand again... Or the voice of reason? At this point, how could she know?

The others were facing the same mental fight, but they had reached the bridge now. It was about six feet wide, which should be okay, only it looked kind of smooth. Was it safe to cross? Andrea was shaking at the thought, but the wand urged her onward. If only it could give her the courage!

"I will attempt the crossing first," Ulric decided. "I am the heaviest here, and if it bears my weight, it will take the rest of you. Wait here."

Andrea was relieved to do just that. Ulric was sweating, and she could almost smell his fear, but he refused to succumb to it. Of course, he was a knight and had trained to face danger and terror. It wasn't something she'd learned in school. It was an integral part of who he was. Instead of giving in to his fear, he walked, somewhat unsteadily, out onto the rock bridge. Slowly, one pace at a time, he crossed over, until he stood on the far side.

"It is easier than it may appear," he called back to them. "You will not fall."

"Want to bet?" Carter muttered. But he steeled himself and started to follow the knight.

"Come on," Blodwen said, gathering her own courage. "Let's go." She gave Andrea a grin that was obviously meant to be comforting, and missed the mark rather badly. Nevertheless, Andrea and her father both followed.

They were halfway across when they heard a flurry of movement, both ahead and behind them. Ulric had been watching them crossing intently, and was caught by surprise. He whirled around, but he was surrounded before he could move. Andrea glanced back, and saw that more of the creatures had slipped from fissures in the rocks where they had hidden till the party had passed.

They were hideous things, vaguely human in shape, but about four feet tall, and stooped. Their legs and arms were long and spidery, bent in odd places. Their bodies were small, and their heads large. They had oversized ears, pointed and hairy, and huge eyes in a shrunken, twisted face. They were a deathly white, and were making low, snuffling sounds. Each of them carried long spears, with nasty-looking points, all of them aimed at one of the travelers.

"What manner of creatures are you?" Ulric demanded of the one closest to him.

The thing croaked, and its voice was reedy and broken. "We be Skellig. You be prisoners."

Chapter Eighteen

Andrea looked around, and realized that they were trapped. Perhaps Ulric could fight, but those on the bridge could not. All the Skellig would have to do was to throw rocks at them until they fell from the bridge into the lava. These creatures had planned their ambush well. She saw Ulric taking all of this in as he sized up their situation.

"It would appear that you are correct," he finally agreed. "It would be foolish of us to try and fight you."

"Foolish," the Skellig agreed. "Surrender?"

"Yes," Ulric said, with a heavy heart.

"Good." The Skellig's mouth twisted in what was clearly meant to be a grin. It exposed a lot of nasty-looking, sharp little teeth. The teeth of a predator...He stared at those on the bridge with his large eyes. "Be coming here."

Faced with no alternative, Andrea and the others edged across the bridge to the far pathway. Immediately, they were surrounded by the Skellig, who kept at a spear's length from them, and alert. The spokesthing took Ulric's torch and threw it into the lava river. "Need no light," he said, snuffling. "Follow."

There was a tunnel in the side of the rock, and the Skellig led their captives within. Without the torch, it soon became darker as they moved further from the lava's glow. Andrea stumbled, finding it difficult to see. "We need a light," she protested.

"No light," the Skellig said firmly. "Glow soon."

Andrea had no idea what he was talking about until a little further down the narrow, confining passageway. Then she saw there was light ahead – pale, thin light, but enough to see by. It seemed to be coming from the walls of the passageway itself.

"Fascinating," her father said. "Some kind of lichen, by the looks of it. Bio-luminescent. I wonder if these Skellig creatures plant it here as a sort of natural light?"

"Do you think they have the brains for it?" asked Carter.

"Skellig smart," the spokesperson said smugly. "Intruders dumb."

"Yeah, but you're ugly," Carter replied.

Andrea touched his arm. "I don't think it's a good idea to get them mad. We're going to need their help."

"Help?" Carter snorted. "We're their *prisoners*. They don't look to me like the kind of... things that help anyone but themselves."

"They have to listen to reason," Andrea said.

Carter eyed the stunted creatures dubiously. "You think they're on speaking terms with reason?"

"We'll soon find out." Andrea marched onward. At least with the lichen light all around them she could see where she was going. The pathway wasn't too long, though they were in some sort of a maze. Tunnels crossed theirs constantly, and anyone who didn't know their way would soon be lost down here. It was obviously another way the Skellig guarded themselves. They clearly didn't like intruders, though Andrea could hardly imagine they'd get many visitors down here.

They emerged eventually into a large, natural cavern. Stalactites and stalagmites adorned the place, and there was more of the glowing moss here. It was horribly low level light, however, much less than moonlight on an overcast night.

In the space were gathered hundreds of the creatures. They were shuffling, scratching and snuffling away to themselves. Andrea felt chilled as those large, blank eyes fixed on her, and the Skellig muttered to themselves. She couldn't make out the words, but the tone was far from friendly.

The cavern was large, hundreds of feet long, and the ceiling was mostly lost in the gloom. They were led across the floor to a huge central stalagmite. This had been carved into the shape of a throne, and one of the Skellig sat here. Unlike the others, who were naked, this one had a robe of some sort of skins and a necklace of what was probably gold about its scrawny throat.

"Intruders," this Skellig hissed. "Forbidden."

"Well, now that we know, we'll just go and stop bothering you," Carter suggested.

"Fool." The Skellig studied them. "Told of intruders, we were.

163

Warned."

Andrea felt a thrill. "My brother?" she asked. "You've seen my brother? He came this way?"

"Brother?" The Skellig shrugged. "Not like you. Friend."

"Oh, great..." Blodwen muttered. She stepped forward. "Look, I don't think you understand. This person you talked with is a great danger to us all. Including you and your people. He has to be stopped. We didn't mean to trespass on your lands, but we are here after him and have to catch and stop him."

"Stop *you*," the Skellig answered, and there was a lot of nasty cackling at this joke. "Friend warned. Kill you."

These creatures seemed to have a very limited understanding, and Mark and the Outwand had obviously duped them into believing that the party was trouble. Andrea winced; how could they win over these monstrosities?

Ulric tried next. "I am a knight," he said simply. "I speak the truth. We are not your foes. We only seek the one who came before us. He wishes to destroy everything – including the Skellig. You must allow us to go after him and prevent death coming to us all."

The Skellig shrugged once more. "Death inevitable," he pointed out. "Lies."

This was not going well. Andrea took a deep breath, and then stepped forward. She held out her wand. "Take this," she suggested. "I have no weapons. If I were an enemy, wouldn't I bring weapons? I only have my guide stick. Take it, feel it. It will tell you that we speak the truth."

The Skellig shied back from the staff. "Trick!" it accused.

"It's *not* a trick!" Andrea said, exasperated. "Why won't you let us explain?"

"They're too scared," her father said. "Wherever we are now, these creatures have lived here, alone, for probably as
long as they know. They don't meet people or much of anything down here. Now we have invaded their space, and they're terrified. They look like monsters to us and we must look like monsters to them. They aren't about to trust us when we speak."

"Great," Carter sighed. "So what do we do, just give up?"

"No." Dr. Ballard moved forward to address the Skellig king. "The one who came before us is my son," he said gently. "I want him back. Can you understand this?" He gestured at the gathered hordes. "You obviously have children of your own. I want my son. Where did he go?"

The Skellig's face writhed as he assimilated this information. Then he gestured off to the far side of the cavern. "Down," he announced. "Tree."

"We're near the World Tree!" Andrea realized. "That's why this is the path the Outwand took. We must be very close behind him."

"Then we have to move now," Blodwen said firmly. "If these creatures won't listen to sense, then we have to act without their help."

"Prisoners!" the Skellig screeched.

"Yes, we are," Blodwen agreed. "For now." She thought for a second, and then looked at Andrea. "Get ready. You and Carter go after Mark. Ulric, your father and I will guard your back. Don't hesitate and don't look back. Stop him."

Andrea didn't understand, but she nodded. Blodwen clearly had a plan of some sort. Gripping her staff, she stood with Carter. Blodwen turned back to the Skellig ruler.

"Will you let us go on in peace?"

"Prisoners!"

Blodwen sighed. "I was afraid you'd say that." She reached into her backpack and pulled out her flashlight. "Now!" she cried, and switched it on, shining it full into the large eyes of the closest Skelligs.

With screams, they threw up their arms to protect themselves. Their large eyes were highly sensitive to the darkness, and they were clearly absolutely blinded and pained
by this. Andrea grabbed Carter's arm and slammed aside the closest of the howling creatures, beating at them with her staff. Carter swung, clearing the way for them to move.

"Go on!" Ulric cried, flinging off the monsters closest to him. "We shall guard your backs, so these creatures cannot follow!"

Andrea hated leaving her father and friends, but knew that she had no choice. The adults were best at fighting, and it was vital that someone stop the Outwand. The Skellig masses grew thinner, and easier to cast aside. Carter was enjoying bashing them, obviously working off his own fears and frustrations. Andrea preferred to push her way. The Skellig were clearly terrified, many rushing blindly out of their way without needing any encouragement. They were clearly not used to fighting, and had little skill at it. Soon, though, they were bound to recollect their courage and try to stop the trespassers. It was important that she and Carter be too far gone by that point. These creatures might not be the best fighters, but they could overcome her and Carter simply by weight of their numbers. And the thought of those nasty, sharp teeth made her shudder.

The staff led her on. It was twisting and writhing in her hand, eagerly on the scent, like a living creature. Mark couldn't be too far ahead of them now! They were closer to finishing this. Unfortunately so, too, was the Outwand. The World Tree was nearby, and it had almost reached its goal.

Andrea plunged into one of the Skellig tunnels. Behind them, she could hear sounds of conflict. Her heart leaped, terrified for her father, Blodwen and Ulric. But she had to trust that they would be fine, able to look after themselves. Right now, even if the others died, she and Carter had to stop the Outwand. No one else could.

"I think we're away from them now," Carter said. He glanced back. "I'm sure they'll be okay."

He was only trying to encourage her, and she wasn't fooled. "The Skellig aren't great fighters," she said. "But there may be thousands of them. Even Ulric can't hold out forever. But we have our job to do, whatever happens."

"Stop your brother, yeah." Carter gave her an odd look. "I'm sorry you're stuck with me; I know you'd prefer to have Ulric here instead."

Andrea gave him a puzzled look. "What are you talking about?"

"Oh, come on. You've got the hots for him, haven't you?"

"You're crazy," she decided. "He's... well, okay, he's brave and handsome and everything. But he's too old for me. *Way* too old, by several hundred years." Now she started to realize why Carter had been acting so strangely. She was amazed she'd been so dense. "Let's face it, can you see him getting into the Mall experience? Taking in a movie? Going to the beach? If there's no monsters to kill, he'd be real gloomy."

"That's true," Carter agreed, sounding better.

"Don't take this the wrong way..." Andrea said. Then she grabbed him and kissed him on the lips. He was too surprised to respond, and she hurried along. A moment later, he caught up with her.

"The wrong way? Hey, how am I *supposed* to take that?"

"Ask me when this is over." She felt almost happy, and she could tell it had made a huge difference to his attitude. "And if you want more where that came from, you'd better take really good care of me."

"Definitely." Carter went quiet again as they hurried along. The light from the Skellig lichen wasn't great, but it was enough for her to see the slight smile on his face. Boys! It was astonishing how easily they could be pleased. And it did seem to have distracted him from his fears and complaints.

The way ahead led downward again, but at least there was no river of fire this time. In fact, it seemed to be growing colder, which was odd. This far underground, the temperature ought to be more or less constant. Instead, it was growing perceptibly colder. Considering how warm it had begun, this wasn't a bad thing – as long as it didn't go too far.

The staff in her hand was almost alive now. It was shaking and sending her waves of conviction. This was *right*! It felt as if it was tugging her along. They were almost there!

Andrea saw her own excitement mirrored in Carter's face. They hurried on, heedless of the poor light. They wanted to get to their goal.

And then they broke through into an immense cavern, larger than any she could have imagined. Distances must be measured in thousands, not hundreds, of feet – and all vertically. It was impossible to see how far upward the cavern extended, and it was difficult to glimpse the far side of it. The center of the cavern was completely occupied by an incredible tree.

Well, actually, not even a whole tree. It was just the roots, digging deeply into the earth all about them. It was impossible to see how far the tree stretched, but it must be more than two or three hundred feet. And it reached above them as far as they could see. The walls of the cavern were glowing with the lichen, illuminating the immense mass of twisted roots. It was massive, warped and unbelievably ancient. She could almost feel the millennia dripping from it.

"Yggdrasil," Andrea breathed. "The World Tree..."

"God," Carter breathed, "I can't see how big this thing is..."

There was the scent of life all about them, but all Andrea could see was a wall of wood, the gnarled, convoluted roots stretching about them. This was a cavern made of myth...

And then one small figure, a hundred feet or so ahead of them.

"Mark!" she screamed. "Mark!"

The figure turned, and then she screamed again, this time in shock and horror.

It was Mark, there was no doubting that. It was still vaguely her brother. But he had *changed* terribly. His right hand clutched the Outwand, which was moving in his grip. His wooden grip... Somehow, Mark had been shaped and altered. His whole body now looked as if it had been carved from wood. His fingers were twigs, his arms branches. His legs were thick trunks, and his feet had been formed into roots, on which he moved unsteadily.

Now she knew what had left those prints they had seen in the dirt earlier – the root-feet he moved upon.

Mark was turning into a tree...

John Peel

Chapter Nineteen

It was hard to believe this creature was still, somewhere inside, her brother. Andrea swallowed. "Mark, what's *happened* to you?"

"Isn't it wonderful?" he cried, raising the Outwand. "I'm whole again! The staff has healed me!"

"Have you *looked* at yourself lately?" Carter asked him incredulously. "You're turning into a scarecrow."

"Side effect, nothing more," Mark answered. "Once the wand has all its power back, it'll heal me completely. Right now its full strength is being blocked."

"Is that what it's told you?" Andrea asked. Mark had stopped to talk, and she and Carter were drawing closer to him. They would soon be within striking distance. "Mark, that thing has *lied* to you!"

"Don't say that!" her brother snarled. "It *healed* me! It did what none of those oh-so-smart doctors could do! It promised to make me whole, and it has done!"

"You think *that's* being whole?" asked Carter. "Wow, your brains must be wooden, too. What are you, Pinocchio in reverse?"

"You always did think you were so clever, Carter Tremaine," Mark snapped. "You're just jealous that the wand picked me and not you!"

"Trust me, I'm glad it didn't latch onto me and try and corrupt my soul," Carter replied. "I like being human, thank you very much."

"Mark," Andrea called. "What do you think is going to happen now you're here? You've reached the World Tree – so what comes next?"

"I destroy it, and Mara gets all of its power back," Mark replied. "The tree is draining it now, preventing it from being whole. Once it has its power back, everything will be fine."

"Everything will be fine – for the Outwand," Andrea explained. "It will have power. But everything else will be destroyed. Mark, the World Tree is what holds reality
together. If it is destroyed, then our world, Annwyn and all of the other levels of reality will no longer be held apart. They'll all merge together and

169

be destroyed."

Mark laughed. "Little sister, somebody's been playing tricks with your mind! That's crazy! Reality can't be held together by a *tree*! I'm only destroying a malignant growth, nothing more." He thought for a moment to try and formulate what he was saying. "It's an invasive species, something that shouldn't be here. It's taking over the whole eco-system of the Earth and other worlds. I have to destroy it to free everything. It's corrupting and infesting all of reality. Can't you see that?" He looked at her plaintively. Even in the wooden face, she could still see conviction.

Then Andrea realized that he was telling the truth: she *had* been duped. He was correct – the idea of a tree, of all things, holding the Universe together was so stupid she was amazed she hadn't realized it before. And she knew how bad invasive species could be, destroying the order of things, fouling everything that they touched. Of course Mark was right – why hadn't she seen it before?

Caliburn blazed in her hand, and she glanced down at it. Slowly the "truth" was cracking under the influence of the good wand. "No!" she screamed. "That's the Outwand, trying to poison my mind again!"

"Yeah, but he is sort of making sense," Carter argued.

"No! We *have* to hold firm. Everything depends upon it."

"But what if he's right?" Carter asked, ashen. "What if we have been lied to? Or just been mistaken? What if what he says is right? That it's just a tree, and nothing more? That it's the infection, what's causing the trouble?"

"It isn't." But even to herself, her voice lacked conviction. Maybe she was wrong...? But she didn't dare waver now, not when everything was so critical. If she was wrong, then so be it; she had to believe that she was right, and act on that conviction. The trouble was that the Outwand was so powerful now that they were this close to it, and the shreds of Caliburn they held so weak...

But the truth was the truth, and she had to clutch onto that...

"Just wait a while and you'll see I'm right," Mark promised her. "As soon as this tree is gone, everything will be fine again." His voice seemed to be getting less and less human, and more like the sound of the wind rustling through the branches. He was losing more and more of his humanity each second.

"I won't let you," she vowed. She was almost up to him now. She could see the grain of the wood in his features now, instead of the texture of skin. There were small leaves already starting to sprout. Was she too late? Was her brother already lost to her?

Carter shuddered. "That story about Merlin being imprisoned in a tree," he said. "It wasn't really like that. He was *turned* into a tree, by the Outwand. It makes everything over into itself."

"Yes," Andrea realized. "It won't heal you when it gains all of its power, Mark — it will absorb you."

"It's not evil," Mark insisted. "You've been lied to. Duped. Mara means only good."

"Really?" Andrea remembered the cat that Mark had been torturing, and how the wand had seemed to be enjoying its pain. "Then you'll have to agree that if it enjoys something wicked, and tries to get you to do something you know is wrong, then it is evil?"

"Of course it would be." Mark sounded puzzled. "But it's made me well, made me walk again. It's led me safely to this spot so that I can free the world from corruption. It's done only good."

Andrea was by his side. "I can prove I'm right," she told him. She could feel a ripple of fear from the Outwand. Could it know what she intended? How could it, when she had only just decided herself? But it was so very powerful and evil...

Mark ignored her, and drew a sword from within his twisted limbs. It was large, ornate and clearly very lethal. It was the sword of a king. It was - *Excalibur...!*

"What do you aim to do?" she asked him, eyeing the blade warily.

"I'm going to destroy the tree," he said.

"With that?" Carter laughed. "It'll take you forever! You'll die of old age before you cut down the World Tree with a sword."

"Not just any sword," Mark said. "Excalibur. The sword which cannot be defeated. Whoever uses it can never fall, and never fail."

"So that's why you took it," Andrea realized. "If you attack the World Tree with Excalibur, it will die, because Excalibur must always win."

171

"Right." Mark was about to step forward. Andrea grabbed at him. She was touching almost pure wood.

"I can prove you've been lied to," she said. "That the Outwand is evil." She reached into her pocket for her penknife, and then opened it up. She hesitated, but knew that everything now depended upon her. She dropped her staff, and raised her left hand, holding it close to the Outwand. Then she plunged the penknife into her palm.

She screamed with the pain of the blow. Carter gasped, and Mark stiffened. Agony lanced through her whole arm as she twisted the blade. She knew she was damaging herself, but there was no option. She had to make the bait irresistible...

The Outwand hummed with pleasure. Wincing in pain, she thrust her hand toward Mark and clutched at the staff, feeling her blood running over it. It fed on pain and suffering, so it must be feasting now. Her hand hurt like the Devil. She was forcing herself to stay clear-headed.

"Now what do you feel?" she gasped through her tears. "Do you feel goodness? Or do you feel Mara feeding from my pain and blood?"

Mark looked shocked, his hand trembling as he held the Outwand. "Kill..." he whispered.

"Yes," she said to him, spilling her blood down the staff and onto his wooden hands. "That's my blood. My life. Mara is drinking it in. And what does the Outwand wish you to do?"

"Kill...." he whispered.

"Yes," she said, grimly. "It wants you to kill me." She looked down at the lethal, naked blade in his other hand. "You've got Excalibur, Mark. It can never fail you. All you need to do is to thrust it into me." She touched her bloody hand to her chest, and winced at the pain. "Just straight through the heart. Or maybe the stomach – that would hurt more, and I'd take longer to die."

"Andrea!" Carter screamed. "What are you doing? He'll *kill* you!"

"That's what the Outwand wants, isn't it, Mark?" Andrea asked, ignoring Carter. "It wants you to take that sword and kill your sister. Doesn't it?"

Mark's face was twisted. "Yes..." His voice was a whisper, his face an abstract carving of wood.

"Is that the good it promised you?" she asked him. "Or is that evil? Can you do it, Mark? Can you kill me to appease that thing? Can you destroy everything, just because it has duped you? It didn't heal you because it's good – it healed you so you could bring it here." She held her hand up again. "Here's my blood, Mark. If you want the rest of it to feed that sick thing that possesses you, then take it."

The Outwand started to scream. Andrea could feel it through her entire body. The taste of her blood was driving it insane. It wanted *more* – it wanted it all. Excalibur twisted in Mark's hand, and the tip of the blade pricked her stomach. Her T-shirt ripped, and a welt of blood formed across her navel. The Outwand was howling now for her blood, determined to drink it all. Mark's whole body contorted as he felt this demand pouring through him. Andrea stared down at the sword that could end her life any second.

Had she pushed too hard? Was the Outwand too strong? Was Mark no longer human enough to understand what was happening? Sweat trickled down her body, and her life hung in the cosmic balance.

With an oath, Mark hurled the Outwand from his grip. Then, screaming, he raised Excalibur in both hands and brought it crashing down on the twisting, writhing staff. Mara cracked apart as the invincible, irresistible blade cleaved through the wooden wand. The Outwand writhed and screamed in their minds. Any other blade than Excalibur – which could never miss its target – would not have been able to hack the wand to pieces. But Mark was furious, and the blade powerful, and in moments, the Outwand's evil influence faded and then died completely.

Panting hard, Mark looked up from the wreckage. "You were right," he whispered. "It *was* evil. It wanted me to kill you, and I just couldn't do that."

Andrea sighed with relief. Her whole body was shaking, but she grabbed her brother, hugging him close. In the end, he had come through. But it was like hugging a tree, there was so little of him now left. "What happens to you now?" she asked, in horror.

"I don't know," Mark admitted. "I guess I'm stuck like this forever..."

"Look on the bright side," Carter suggested weakly. "Trees live a lot longer than people. Maybe you will, too."

Andrea didn't even want to think about it. She retrieved her own staff, feeling a great need for support. "I think we've done what we came for," she said, looking around. "Yggdrasil is safe, the worlds won't collide, and Mark is still alive – even if he's changed. Mara is finally destroyed, and Excalibur recovered. And I really don't want to spend any more time underground than I have to. Plus, we have to go help Dad, Ulric and Blodwen."

"Who's Blodwen?" Mark asked. "And Ulric?"

"A really neat lady we know," Andrea said. "And he's one of Arthur's knights."

"I remember Arthur," Mark confessed, as they started walking back. He shuffled rather than walked, as his legs weren't bending quite right, stiff as they were. "That's where I stole Excalibur..." He looked down at the legendary sword. "I guess I really should give it back."

"It might still come in handy," Carter suggested. "We've still got the Skellig to face..."

"Oh, yeah, them." Mark grimaced, and his face sounded like creaking wood. "I caused some trouble with them, didn't I?"

"Oh yes," Andrea agreed. "Now we have to hope that the others survived it."

"Trouble..." Carter warned, and fell back to join them.

In the opening ahead that led back to the Skellig warrens, dozens of shifting, darting forms were moving. Andrea gripped her staff, ready to fight, and Mark moved to the front of the group, Excalibur raised.

"This is my fault, guys," he apologized. "I'll face the music."

The Skellig spilled silently from the tunnel, blocking their way. Andrea's throat went dry. Did this mean they'd overrun the adults and killed them? If so, it was unlikely that the three of them would get out of this alive...

And then Ulric strode forward, his sword sheathed, and a slight smile on his face. "Don't worry," he said. "The Skellig are on our side now."

"There's a turnabout," Carter muttered.

Blodwen and Dr. Ballard came forward. "We felt the Outwand screaming," Blodwen explained. "Its baleful effects lessened, and the Skellig came to their senses. They realized they'd been tricked."

"Trickster," said the Skellig ruler, pointing at Mark.

"It's okay," Andrea called, hastily. "He's free now. The Outwand is destroyed."

"Good Lord!" Dr. Ballard gasped. "What happened to you, Mark?"

"We'll explain later," Andrea promised. "Look, would anybody really mind if we got out of here? I'm getting the creeps staying underground this long. I want fresh air and light."

"Me too," Blodwen agreed firmly.

"Good," the Skellig grumbled. "Intruders go. Skellig stay."

"Yes, I'll bet you'll be glad to see the back of us, too," Andrea said. "You'll have your privacy back when we're gone."

"Fine," the Skellig agreed.

The way back was a lot simpler than the way down. Several of the Skellig went with the party – probably more to make sure they actually left than to guide them. They retraced their steps with the aid of the urgings of Caliburn until they stood at the place where they had descended from Annwyn. Here the Skellig simply abandoned them, vanishing back into their tunnels without even a word of farewell. They would be happy now they were left alone again.

"Now what?" Carter asked.

Andrea had no doubts. With the Outwand destroyed, her mind was clear once again. No more hesitation, no more confusion. Well, at least no more than usual! She struck her staff against the wall of earth ahead of them. There was another flow of power, and then the ground opened up once more. Light streamed down at them. They all blinked, dazzled by real light at long last, and then stepped out into the hall of the Lady of the Lake.

They were instantly surrounded by knights and ladies, all talking at once, asking questions and laughing. The Lady cleared her throat – quietly, but everyone immediate shut up. She stepped forward and looked at them, her face radiant.

"The Outwand has been destroyed," she said. It wasn't a question. "Its effects are dying away already. The worlds are moving farther apart, safe once again."

"Apart?" Andrea felt a sudden panic. "Uh, it's not that I don't like this place, but I *really* would like to get home while it's still possible."

"I understand, child, but don't worry. We have the strength to pass you all back to your homes. But not before you have been properly thanked." The Lady clapped her hands. "I have never heard of a better reason for a feast than this!"

That galvanized everyone into action. A couple of the ladies grabbed Andrea and dragged her away. The others were likewise whisked off. The next hour or so was a blur in her mind, because it started with a warm bath, and she'd have happily stayed there forever. But she was rudely forced out by the laughing ladies, and then given fresh clothes to wear. Considering the state of her T-shirt and jeans, she was grateful for this. Her wound was dressed, and her hand felt a little better now, though it still throbbed badly. Still, the pain was a small price to pay.

Andrea took one look at the clothing she was offered, and started getting selective. "I want my own underwear back," she said firmly. There was no way she was wearing the medieval version – it looked like something from a torture chamber. But she happily accepted the beautiful flowing blue dress. The ladies fixed her hair for her, twining in flowers, and then she was finally led to the feast.

Chapter Twenty

The hall was so packed with tables that looked almost ready to collapse under the weight of all of the food. Andrea was astonished at the pies, pastries, meats, fowl, fruits, breads, and vegetables. The delicious scents were overpowering, and her stomach reminded her of how long it had been since she had last eaten. The Lady of the Lake was seated at the head, and waved Andrea to a place on her left.

Blodwen was already there, looking beautiful in her own flowing red gown. Ulric was beside her, tidied and happy. Dr. Ballard, looking slightly uncomfortable in flowing scholar's robes, and Carter – red-faced in his own page's uniform – were waiting for her. And then there was Mark.

Andrea blinked. He looked slightly different, less wooden. Not human, exactly, but a lot closer to it than she was sure he had been. He nodded confirmation.

"With the destruction of the Outwand, its power over me is waning," he said happily. "I'm changing back once again. You stopped it in time. Thank you, sis."

"I'm glad." Andrea found herself blushing as he helped her to her seat.

And then the feast began. Half of the time, Andrea wasn't sure what she was eating, but it all tasted wonderful. Partly, that was due to sheer relief, she knew, and partly because she was so hungry. And partly simply because it felt so good to be able to be happy and rejoice again. With Mara destroyed that oppressive gloom and uncertainty was gone. There were minstrels, tumblers, and speeches from anyone who felt like giving one. Andrea was content to stay on the sidelines and enjoy it all.

Eventually, though, it was over. The Lady of the Lake clapped her hands and called for the servants to clean the tables. "There are still things for us to do," she said to them, privately. "First of all, there is Excalibur." She looked at Mark. "It must be returned to its rightful owner."

"Of course." Mark had the sword ready.

"*You* must return it," the Lady informed him, "for you were the one who took it."

They went into the tunnels again. This time, they didn't seem quite as gloomy of depressing. The Waiting Place was guarded, but the knights moved to allow the party to enter. The Lady led the way to Arthur's stone bed, and they all watched as Mark gently replaced Excalibur into its empty scabbard.

"One thing I don't get," Carter said. "You know, Arthur's supposed to sleep till some great emergency wakens him and brings him back to help England. We've just faced the possible destruction of all life in every world – and he slept through it like a baby. If *that* wasn't enough to wake him – what will?"

Andrea shuddered at the thought. "I don't think I want to know the answer to that," she confessed.

They returned to the Lady's reception hall, where Andrea discovered their wands of Caliburn were laid on the floor, awaiting them. "Now, I think," the Lady said, "is the time for you to return to your own world. We none of us here shall ever forget what you have done."

Andrea felt a slight pang. It would be good to return home, but it would be sad as well. She could get used to this lifestyle... maybe. But no Malls, no cinemas, no CDs...? Maybe not!

Ulric moved to join the Lady. "I, of course, shall be staying here," he said. "This is my home." He was carefully not looking at anyone as he said this, which puzzled Andrea. She was going to miss the knight; over the past few days, she'd grown very fond of him. But why couldn't he look at them?

Blodwen moved forward, her face slightly flushed. "I'm thinking of putting in for a transfer," she said, looking at the Lady and not at Ulric. "Do you think there's room here for a police woman?"

"There is always a welcome for a valiant heart," the Lady said warmly. She looked pointedly at Ulric, who had cheered up immensely. "And, I suspect, more than a simple welcome."

"What do you know?" Carter muttered. "I think we've got a love match here..."

Andrea laughed. She'd never suspected it, despite all of the signs. Now she knew how Blodwen had ended up with Ulric's knife..."I think they'll both be very happy. This is, after all, a fairy tale castle, and here they always live happily ever after..." Then she rushed to hug Blodwen. "I'll miss you." Blodwen winced, and Andrea let her go, realizing her back must still be tender."Sorry."

"I'll miss you all, too," Blodwen said, sadly. "I've gotten quite used to you."

"It may not be a permanent separation," Ulric said. "The Outwand is destroyed, but Caliburn still exists. And the Lady Andrea still has her amulet that can breach the worlds, as well as the power within herself to use it. It may be possible for you to return when the time is right."

"All right!" Carter said. Then he caught himself. "I mean, it would be great to see you guys again sometime."

"But for now," the Lady said, "I think that it is time you returned to your own world. There are people there who must know that this is all over. And much work for you all there, I fear. But go knowing you have friends here in Annwyn who value the service you have done."

Andrea's eyes were misting at this, and she picked up one of the wands quickly, before she broke down. She clutched at the amulet, and then reached out. She felt the power flowing through her, and then there was a gap in the air before them, leading not to a stone wall but to a bright summer sky. "Goodbye," she called, and stepped through. Her father, brother, and Carter, all with their own wands, followed.

There was a deep baying sound, and then a huge shape was upon her. Andrea barely had time to panic before a huge tongue licked across her face. She pushed at the mass. "Caldera! Down, boy!"

The hound obediently retreated a pace, and she hugged him tightly. "It's good to see you, too. You've been waiting all of this time?" Caldera nodded, looking happily at her.

Carter grunted. "I suspect you've got yourself a pet. Herne won't take him back now – he's almost tame." Caldera growled. "Hey, I said *almost*!"

"You could be right there." Andrea glanced around. They were standing on the summit of the Tor again, but this time the air was fresh and clear. There were no overlaps from other realities, and the ghosts had all vanished once again. The crowds seemed to be slowly dissipating.

People were talking to one another, uncertainly, as if recounting a strange dream. Would all of this somehow soon be forgotten? Perhaps everything was returning to normal?

"I guess it's time to take Carter home," Dr. Ballard said. "His parents have to be very worried."

"We can call them from the village, dad," Andrea pointed out. "I think electricity will be back on now."

"Right," Mark agreed. "He looked almost fully human again now. Then he stumbled and fell, his face ashen. "My legs!"

His father whipped down beside him. "What's wrong?" he asked, anxiously.

"I can't walk," Mark said softly. "It was the Outwand that cured me. But, like the other effects, it's worn off again."

"I am so sorry," Andrea said, bending down beside him.

"I'm not." Mark sounded strangely content. "You know, I've discovered that there are a lot worse things in life than not being able to walk. A lot worse. All in all, I'll settle for what I am." He grinned at her. "And for having one terrific sister."

Andrea's heart felt very full, and she was definitely in danger of crying now. "We'll help you down," she said.

"I'm almost looking forward to my wheelchair again," he confessed.

With Carter's help, she linked hands, and they carried Mark between them. Carter gave her a funny look. "There's one more thing," he said. "That kiss..."

"Kiss?" Mark asked.

Andrea blushed. "Uh, yeah... Look, Carter, that was just to encourage you, you know. You were depressed, and needed cheering up. It didn't mean anything."

"Didn't it?" Carter asked, studying her flushed face. "Really?"

Andrea didn't really want to start exploring *that* issue. "We'll talk about it later," she suggested.

"Oh, yes," Carter agreed. "We will indeed."

Life, it seemed, was back to normal.

It felt glorious.

About the Author

John Peel was born in England and moved to the U.S. in 1981 to get married. He and his wife live on Long Island with their pack of miniature pinschers. He has written over a hundred books, including the "2099" series and "Dragonhome", along with tie-ins based on "Doctor Who", "Star Trek" and "The Outer Limits".

You can find him at:

www.john-peel.com

and on Facebook at www.facebook.com/JohnPeelAuthor

Also from Dragonhome Books

The Slayers of Dragonhome (ISBN 9780615567082)

The sequel to the popular *The Secret of Dragonhome*!

Melayne is still in trouble – lots of it. Her brother wants her dead. Sea-Raiders are trying to kill her. Her dragons are growing up and want mates. Her husband is missing. And then the dragon slayers arrive in force…

Forced to fight to protect everyone and everything she loves, Melayne must abandon her family and chase down answers. It seems that all roads are leading back to Dragonhome. But what awaits her there apart from a deadly family reunion? And what is the terrible danger from her distant past?

Book of Time & Book of Games (ISBN 9780615726007)

The next two volumes in the "Diadem" series!

Shanara decides to reveal her history to Score, Helaine, Pixel and Jenna in her own unique way – by creating a realistic illusion from her memories. But a powerful sorcerer hijacks her spell and transports the five of them back into the past instead. Now instead of seeing Shanara's troubled story, they are forced to live it. But if they change anything – anything at all – they might wipe out the future… including themselves.